SAVING SUMMER

Florida Veterans Book 1

TIFFANI LYNN

Happy Reading!

Saving Summer

Florida Veterans Book One

Tiffani Lynn

Acknowledgments

As always, my first thanks goes out to my husband and amazing daughters. Making you guys proud is what I strive for. Love you always.

I'm lucky to have a ton of support when it comes to the author side of my life. Special thanks go to Judy Swinson, Kat Mizera, Katharina LeBoeuf and Lexi Post. I love you guys and appreciate the special friendship we share. This would be so much harder without you.

To my TLC Crew... Dilly Dilly and What you find is what you find. I love you guys and cherish the memories we have together even if the teasing is relentless.

Wolfpack... For you guys I will continue to wear some kickass pant suits. Be prepared for full awesomeness.

To my readers, thank you for your time and kindness. Your support means the world to me.

Dedication

To April Klusman, my sister-in-law and friend. You were one of the first people to read my work and encourage me to share it. I can't thank you enough for all you do for me and my family. I love and appreciate you more than I can express!

1

Summer

_____

The warmth of Mike's hand on the bare skin of my thigh wakes me. My short flippy rayon skirt has hiked up and is higher than is polite on an airplane. It must have ridden up while I was asleep, so I reach to pull it down, and he stills my hand. *What?* I look up from where my head is resting on his shoulder.

"Are you cold?" he asks, and it's then that I notice his eyes burning with something unfamiliar.

"A little," I confess. He reaches over to the empty seat on my right and grabs the lap blanket, spreading it out over both our legs. Then, he moves his hand underneath the blanket and back to the same location on my thigh. In the 34 years I've known Mike Wade, he's never touched me so . . . intimately. I rest my head on his shoulder again and close my eyes, trying to figure out why his hand is there and why I'm enjoying it so much. The light, swirling patterns his fingers are making cause chills to race down my legs and up my arms. I shiver a little and, without thought, spread my legs some to give him better access as he continues to move a little higher. His body heaves with the breath he sucks in at my reaction to his touch.

For the remaining 30 minutes of our flight from Denver home to Tampa, he brings a slow burn to my core as he works all the way up my thigh, just shy of my panty line. By the time the plane comes to a stop at the gate, I'm so hot and bothered I could mount and ride him all the way to my happy place in front of everyone on this plane. Have I ever been this turned on? Especially when there's no making out or heavy petting? At 42 years old, it seems sad that my answer is no. I've never been this turned on by such a small gesture.

Mike and I have been friends—best friends—for years, but he's never touched me like this before. I've also never been as aware of him as I am now. Well, that may not be true, but this is the first time I can tell he's feeling the same thing, and for once, neither of us is hiding it. What brought this on?

As we exit the plane, Mike places his hand on the small of my back and doesn't remove it until we reach the busy portion of the airport where everyone lines up to go through security. Maybe he's just looking for comfort after we left his sister—our other best friend—Valerie, crying at the gate in Denver. It was a dramatic scene—in fact, the whole week was rough as we helped her get settled after her husband left, taking their 11-year-old daughter with him.

In all the years of my friendship with Mike, I've tried to bury the crazy attraction I've had to him, an effort that right now seems stupid. I have my reasons, and they still make sense to me, but tonight I don't want to pretend I don't feel the desire for him. In fact, I'm about half a second from asking him to come back to my place. It's been a while since I've been with anyone and probably forever since I was with a man who could actually light my fire without effort.

At this stage in life, I don't have interest in sexual encounters with men who don't turn me on. I'd rather grab my vibrator and take care of business myself than to fake a reaction I don't feel. The problem, though, is I learned a long time ago to stay away from the men who *really* turn me on because they always break your heart in the worst ways and I can't deal with that. My mother and father are good examples of this. She fell for him hook, line and sinker. They burned hot and they burned bright just long enough to conceive me, and then he left her high and dry with a newborn and a severely broken heart. I'm pretty certain she never quite recovered from it.

We stop by baggage claim and grab our suitcases. The reminder of broken hearts has me ready to ignore my reaction to him on the airplane and say goodbye when he says, "Summer, come on. I'm taking you home."

"It's okay. My place is out of your way, and I'm sure you have work tomorrow." I pull my phone from my purse and begin typing. "I'm already pulling up Uber."

"Don't argue, and no, I don't have work tomorrow. It wouldn't matter if I did, though. Wait here so I can bring my truck around. I'm on the top level and you'll get soaked the way this rain is coming down."

"I've never melted before. I'll be fine." He's hilarious. There's nothing high-maintenance about me. I'm not the kind of girl to worry about messing up my hair or getting my clothes a little wet, and he knows this better than anyone. He starts to argue with me, but I ignore it and cross the covered walkway, wheeling my suitcase behind me. The elevator ride up is quiet and tense, which is a completely new feeling between us.

When the door opens on the top level, I look out to find that it's no longer raining—it's now coming down like a waterfall in sheets of water. *Shit.* I unzip the top of my suitcase and shove my purse down inside—not wanting to get my phone or personal items wet—then turn to Mike and say, "I'll follow you." He glances down at my white tank top and back at my face and grins. Sometimes he reminds me of the teenager he used to be, playful and flirty. God, I love this side of him, always have. Something about his youthful reaction sends a jolt of fire to my nipples and they harden beneath my shirt.

"Damn," I mutter, realizing that I'm about to be on full display in my white tank top, but unwilling to back down now. I'll never hear the end of it if I do.

As he darts out into the rain, I follow him down three aisles, in and out of a few cars, and back up to the side of the first row we passed. That joker took us the long way on purpose. He drops the tailgate on his truck and shoves both of our bags into the covered bed. I turn to hurry around to the front passenger side when he grabs me and pulls me to him. I blink away the water in my eyes as the rain continues to pour. When he spins me to face him, I crane my neck back because he's a good foot taller than me. His eyes are heated in a way I've never seen aimed at me. My breath catches as he lowers his mouth to mine and slides his arms around my waist, pulling me tight against his body.

When our lips connect, it's like nothing I've ever felt before. Desire unfurls in my belly, sending tingles throughout my body and blocking any rational thought. My sex throbs between my legs, and I have the sudden desire to slip my hand between us and relieve the ache that he started. Between the long emotional week, his touch on the plane, and the fantasy-like quality of this whole scene, the kiss turns wild more quickly than it normally would, and I can feel his cock harden against my stomach. *Holy hell.*

With my palms on both sides of his face, I hold him to me and I'm not sure why. It's almost as if I can't get close enough, like I'm trying to climb inside him or meld us together. Our kiss keeps changing direction, our mouths moving with and against each other, like it's brand-new, but, at the same time, like we've been doing this forever. I can't explain it.

Without hesitation, his hand moves up under my shirt while his fingers find my nipple through my flimsy bra. He circles the peak roughly before he pinches and rolls it. I break the kiss, moaning, "Mike . . ." I can't help but shiver a little and he steps back.

"Cold?" he asks.

I shake my head and say, "More," loud enough to be heard over the pounding of the rain. His eyes burn into me like he's trying to figure out if this is real. My tongue snakes out and slides across my bottom lip as he contemplates my reaction. His grin from a few minutes ago returns, and he grabs my hand, pulling me to the passenger side of his truck. He opens the door, slides the seat back and climbs in. Task completed, he leans over to tug me inside onto his lap. I pull the door shut, and I find myself in the position I wanted to be in on the plane —center-to-center, chest-to-chest and face-to-face. My skirt is pushed up near my hips, exposing a sliver of my white lace panties. I'm dripping all over his truck, and it's obvious he couldn't care less that we're ruining his leather seats. Before things can get awkward, he grabs the hem of my blouse, whipping it over my head, and with equal efficiency, he pops the front clasp of my bra, allowing my breasts to break free. Quickly, he slips the straps off my shoulders and cups both breasts in his hands. The look in his eyes is hungry, feeding the growing fire within me.

He's so damn handsome. Just the width and obvious strength of his shoulders is hot and that doesn't account for the perfectly muscled pecs and abs I've been admiring since he was 17 years old and working out every day. The look on his face is probably similar to mine, and instead of feeling self-conscious, I feel sexy and free.

"I've dreamt of what these would look like for years, and now I can't get enough," he whispers, tracing the underside curve of my breast with his fingertips. "Every time you came out to the pool or the lake wearing a bikini, I'd get hard thinking about what your nipples looked like behind those tiny triangles of fabric."

"Mike," I say, my voice quiet and breathy. He groans as he lifts my breast in his palm, swiping his tongue across the sensitive nipple as another pulse of heat sweeps through me, ending at my pussy. I rock a little against him while he takes one of my nipples into his mouth, lightly scraping it with his teeth and finishing with a suckle of pure pleasure. He repeats the process on the other nipple, and I can't take the wait any longer. I need some relief *now*, so I slip my hand between us, into my panties and find my clit. As soon as I make contact, I gasp. He drops his gaze from mine to watch what my fingers are doing and he groans.

"Slip a finger inside. I want to watch," he says. Then he hooks the front of my panties, holding them down so he can watch as I bury my finger in my pussy, as deep as it can go in this position. My head falls back as I slide it in and out slowly. This feels so good, and it's hot as hell because he's watching. With a firm grip on my wrist, he pulls my hand away and up to his mouth. Before I can react, he closes his lips around the wet digit and sucks it clean. I lean forward and roll my hips a little, doing my best to find friction against his pants. He releases my hand and cups both of my breasts, pinching and teasing the nipples, driving me to the brink of insanity. I can't take it. I need to feel him inside me, I need to ride this feeling all the way through. I need . . . I need . . . I need *him*. Now.

"Fuck me," he groans.

"Yes, yes, now," I beg. He doesn't waste any time digging for his wallet while I go back to fingering myself in front of him.

"Hold on, M, you've got to lift up," he tells me.

The use of the nickname he gave me as a kid reminds me of how well I know him, but also how little I know him like *this*, as a virile, sexy man capable of making me beg for sex in an airport parking lot. I brace myself on the seat, one hand on each side of his head, and lift my body so he can shove his wet shorts down his legs to the floor. The most magnificent cock I've ever seen juts between us, leaning slightly to the left, proud and hard. The dark nest of curls at the base is matted down against his skin from the damp fabric that was pressed against it. I know I've never been with anyone as big as he is, and I'm dying to know how it feels to be stretched that far, for him to be buried deep.

Once he has the condom on, I lower myself onto his thick cock while he takes my nipple into his mouth again. I must be moving too slowly because he grips my hips and pulls me down hard, causing us both to cry out. I can't help the flutter of my pussy around him. I'm already so close, and the fullness of him is almost more than I can handle. The windows are fully fogged now, and the truck is sweltering with our hormonal heat. I tug on his shirt, getting him to pull it over his head and drop it to the floorboard. His muscled chest is damp, yet warm, as I lean in against him, seeking more contact.

"M, your pussy is so fucking tight. Squeeze me, move on me, do something; I can't take it, you feel so damn good." His naughty words urge me on farther. I rise and fall on him, my muscles aching with the effort in this cramped position, but I'm unable to stop and forced forward by lust and desire, in a mixture more potent than I've ever experienced. He traps one of my breasts as it bounces in front of him and takes it with his teeth. He tests my pain tolerance by biting down slowly; and the harder he goes, the more my pussy contracts. I love a little pain with my pleasure. Of course, none of the men I've been with have been willing to take it far enough.

When his hand slips between us and his fingers find my engorged clit, pressing down and circling, I spiral over the edge, screaming his name. If anyone is walking through this parking lot, I know they'll think I'm being murdered. Even if they call the cops, it'll be worth the orgasm he just gave me. I've never come that hard before. My heart is still racing wildly, moisture from the rain mixes with my sweat while I brace myself on either side of his shoulders. Our eyes are locked as he relentlessly pounds into me, chasing his own completion. Every muscle in his body pulls tight only seconds before the tension releases, and I feel his cock pulse inside me as he empties himself into the condom. I finally allow myself to collapse and rest my head on his broad shoulder.

All these years, I've avoided looking at him as more than a friend and, in this moment, I can't remember why. Don't get me wrong, over the years I noticed every new muscle that popped up, and every inch he gained in height. On occasion, I wondered what it would be like to kiss lips as full as his, but I tried to keep the thought process there. How do we go back to being best friends? Can I even pretend not to think of his enormous cock while he tells me about his mom's job or the new trick his dog can do? I think I'm screwed in more ways than one.

"Summer," he says quietly, and I groan a little. I don't want to go back to reality. I want to stay comfortable and warm, with his cock buried inside me while we're pelvis-to-pelvis in his truck.

"Look at me, M. Don't make me go back to being just your friend yet. I have a few days before I go back to work. Come spend that time with me. Please."

He doesn't phrase it like a question, it's more of a statement. I lean back and study his expression. It's what I want, but will that make things worse when we go back to real life? If we part right now, can we pretend none of this happened?

"Did we just ruin our friendship?" I ask, scared of his response.

"God, I hope so. I've always wanted to be more than your friend, M."

"Mike . . ."

"Don't give me the million excuses I'm sure you're brewing up as to why you need to go back to the nerd-herd of guys you date. Give me this weekend. Please. Let me prove to you how good we can be together. I've always wanted this chance." His arms close around me, and I'm powerless to resist.

"Take me to your place," I whisper, half in fear and half in anticipation.

2

Summer

By the time we get readjusted, with him in the driver's seat and me in the passenger seat, it's 10 minutes later. It's taken another couple of minutes to defog the windows so he can see out of them well enough to drive. Throughout that time we're quiet. Maybe I should have him take me home. Without my hormones in overdrive to guide my thought process, I'm starting to think this is a bad idea.

Mike and I have spent 34 years enjoying a successful friendship, and it's been one of the most important relationships of my life; I can't imagine throwing it all away for a few days between the sheets with him. If his sister, Valerie—my best friend for an equal number of years—gets wind of this, she'll question my sanity. We were like the three musketeers growing up, and the idea of breaking our group up is overwhelming. Because there's no way I'll ever look at him the same again. No way I'll ever be able to see him with another woman and not want to get in a high school-style catfight over him. I've had jolts of jealousy when I've seen him with various women over the years but have always been able to keep that in check. I won't be able to after this.

"Stop fidgeting, M. Shut off your mind and go with it," he says, his voice low but soft.

"How'd you know my mind is whirling?" I turn as far as the seat belt will permit and face him.

He reaches out, his fingers gently stroke under my chin and pause to hold me in place. "I know everything about you. Don't overthink this. Please, just give me this weekend." The blue of his eyes is deeper than it was earlier and something I see in their depths settles me.

"Okay," I whisper. He leans over and presses his lips to mine softly before putting the truck in gear and driving us to his place.

When we pull into the driveway I notice a light on in the living room and an unfamiliar car is in the driveway. "Did you hire a Scooter-sitter?" I ask, referring to his basset hound. *Who would be at his house this late?*

"Yup, but that's not who's here." He doesn't elaborate, but I can see the instant tension in his shoulders and the tic in his jaw.

He grabs both of our bags and carries them to the door, where he sets them down. Before he unlocks it, he turns to me. "There's nothing going on with Tawney. I hired her sister, Tabby, to watch Scooter. I don't know why she's here, so give me a few minutes to get this straight. Don't read into it, no matter what she says."

Great. We aren't even a few hours into this, and I'm already going to want that high school-style throwdown. I'm not even a fighter. I've never been aggressive, but if I were a cat right now, the hair on my back would be standing on end. I sigh and nod.

"Let's get this over with."

When the door opens, Scooter greets Mike with several loud barks and a nudge to the shins. Mike sets the bags inside and shuts the door behind me. Then he bends over and gives the overweight basset hound a full-body rubdown, pausing to get a spot right above his tail that he loves so much. Then he stands and looks around. No Tawney anywhere.

I've only met her once, and I'm not a fan. She's model material and about 10 years younger than we are. Beautiful on the outside, but rotten black on the inside. Our last encounter didn't go well. Valerie was in town for a visit right before she left for her last deployment, and we were having a cookout with their parents and their brother, Thomas, here at Mike's house when she showed up uninvited. He'd been sleeping with her and she wanted more, so she decided to force a meeting with the family. Tawney and I hated each other on sight. By the time the day was over, she'd made a scene and he'd ended the affair. I thought she was gone from his life, but apparently not.

"Tawney," Mike yells into the house.

Within seconds she appears at his bedroom doorway in a skimpy little negligee. I'll give her credit—she has a fantastic body. It's long and lean with curves in the right places. Although, I'm certain she got a boob job at some point because those are sitting a little too high for the size they are. Looking at her in that outfit makes me feel older than my 42 years. She looks young, vibrant and supple. I feel like an old saggy version of that. She's smiling at him like he's dinner until I come into view. Her eyes narrow on me, and she places a hand on her hip.

"What's she doing here?" Tawney questions Mike and then she turns to me. "Don't you have your own house?"

I cross my arms over my still wet chest and glare at her. If I open my mouth, the words coming out will be nasty and mean.

"She's my guest, Tawney, unlike you. Where's Tabby?" I can tell she's reworked whatever plan she had cooked up in her head because I can see the change in her demeanor immediately. Her lush bottom lip turns pouty, and she almost absently runs a long red claw of a fingernail over the swell of her right boob. She's using her best assets to grab Mike's attention.

"She's sick. She said she left you a message. Flu or something. She didn't want to leave Scooter to fend for himself, so she sent me here yesterday. I thought you might like a nice little welcome home."

When she's done with her little show, I want to puke or punch her. I'm not sure which urge is greater.

"I brought my welcome home with me," he tells her, and she jerks back like she's been slapped.

Tawney's overly made-up eyes bulge out of her head, and she throws her hand out toward me. "Summer? Really? She's like 50 years old or something. It's gross."

Her lip curls in disgust and I lunge for her. "Bitch! I'm not 50!" is all I can think to say. I need to get better with the comebacks. Calling a woman older than her age is an insult and she knows it.

Mike grabs me and pulls me against him. Low, but clearly, he says, "Summer's not 50. She's younger than I am, actually. Besides, you won't meet a more beautiful woman than Summer. Grab your shit and get out. Don't come back. I don't care if the zombie apocalypse starts and you're the only person left alive, I don't ever want to see you again. You aren't welcome here."

She stomps toward his bedroom, and he releases me to follow her, watching from the doorway as she packs. I squat down and scratch Scooter's belly while I wait. I'm furious, but Mike's words have soothed the sting of her nasty words a little.

3

Mike

Fucking Tawney. The only reason she was ever around was to keep my dick from getting lonely, but I knew she wasn't the right one for me. She may be hot as hell on the outside, but she's a viper on the inside. I don't like people like that and refuse to associate with them. The only reasons I used Tabby this time to watch Scooter were because my parents were out of town, my neighbor was unavailable and I was in a hurry to get to Valerie. I really like Tabby, she's the sweet one in her family—not my type, but sweet—but she's a last resort.

I watch as Tawney is angrily shoving shit in her bag and mumbling as she goes. Once she zips up the suitcase, she pauses to glare at me. "Really? Her? I knew you had something going with her. You're an idiot. You could have this." She gestures to her body, now covered in short shorts and a barely-there tank top. "Instead you picked her. She's one day away from menopause. In a few weeks, she'll be shriveled like a raisin, all dried up and wrinkled. Good luck with that."

Heaving her suitcase off the bed, she drags it past me and out the door, her perfume burning my eyes in her wake. I never respond to her wrinkle comment because it doesn't warrant such. She's just being a bitch. She's so vain that she doesn't see anything past the 17 layers of makeup someone like her wears.

Tawney leans back in the door and says, "Oh, and one more thing, Mike. I hate your fat-ass dog, so don't expect me or my sister to ever take care of him again." After that parting remark she slams the door behind her.

I turn to see Summer sitting on the floor by my couch, rubbing Scooter's belly like she had the entire time Tawney packed. Summer's hair is damp from the rain, her makeup a little smudged, and her clothes are wet and wrinkled. I take a deep breath and move across the room toward her, my eyes never leaving hers. When I reach her, I bend down and take her hand to help her up. She stands and I tug her in for a kiss. It starts slow, just a peck at first. I slide my fingers into the hair at the sides of her head and open my mouth enough so she knows what I want. Her lips part and her tongue slips out to greet mine. I change direction and kiss her harder, tangling our tongues and nipping at her lower lip. A sweet little moan slips from her mouth and I decide to move this to the bedroom, so I scoop her up and carry her to my bed.

When we approach my room, the scent of Tawney's perfume is still heavy. "Let's get rid of this stench," I tell her with a wicked grin.

"Want me to get the spray from the bathroom?" she asks.

I shake my head. "Nope, I want to replace it with the scent of our sex and *your* perfume," I explain as I strip off my wet shirt and drop my wet shorts and boxers to the floor.

"I don't wear perfume anymore."

"Well, I guess that means we need to double up on the sex to get rid of that nasty shit." Before she can say something else, I grip the hem of her shirt and whip it over her head, like I did in the truck, and send it to the floor.

A gentle push to her shoulder sends her to her back, and I grip the rayon skirt and give it a little tug.

"Wait, it has a zipper," she tells me before lowering it. I pull the skirt off her body and drop it with the shirt. "Can you turn off the light?" she asks, her voice quieter than usual.

"No." Is she crazy? I want to watch.

"Please?" she begs.

I pull away from her neck, where I had started kissing a line downward to her heavy breasts, to look at her. "Why? I want to see you."

She won't look at me and now she's gnawing on her thumbnail like she always does when she's nervous or concerned, and I know exactly what happened. Tawney, with her old-lady comments. "Don't listen to Tawney."

I grip her wrists, pull them above her head and hold them in place with one hand while the other trails down over her hair, her cheek, her throat, traveling the ample curve of her breast along the bra, down over her belly—which only has a slight roundness to it—and finally arriving at her panty line. I slip my fingers inside and through the folds to find the heated center of her.

She fights against the restraint of my hand. "Hold still, M. I'm gonna fuck you with my fingers and I plan to watch." Her body quivers and her eyes dart away from me.

"Mike," she says, almost breathless.

"God, Summer, since I was 17 years old, I've been jerking off to thoughts in my head of you like this. I want to see the real thing—live. Please let me leave the light on." My pointer finger swirls over her swollen clit. I know how to manipulate to get what I want and I really want this. Her legs open farther and her hips rotate to follow my motion. "Lights?" I ask. I swirl faster with a tad more pressure.

"Yes, yes, yes, just don't stop," she moans.

I lean down to kiss her, a smile still plastered to my mouth. "Leave your hands above your head." When I remove my hand and grip her tiny panties on each side, tugging hard, I rip the flimsy material.

"Mike!" she scolds.

"I'll buy you more," I tell her as I lower my head between her legs. She grabs a pillow and tucks it under her head, her eyes now trained on mine as I take the first taste of her sweet pussy. The salty tang of her arousal coats my tongue, and I hum with satisfaction, ready for more. My mouth explores her tender folds slowly, dipping inside her every so often, and then returning to concentrate on her clit. As it swells, and her body jerks with the first tremors of orgasm, I slip two fingers inside her and curl inward a little to find that perfect spot. I work her hard and fast, unable to control myself. As her neck finally arches and her pussy flutters before clenching tight, I make sure to watch her facial expressions through it all. It's even more amazing than I've ever dreamed up myself. Her mouth is set in the perfect O, eyes clenched tight and her neck is arched as far back as it will go.

I pull my fingers from within her and slip them into my mouth to savor the delicious nectar while she watches. It's like I'm obsessed with the taste of her. Then I reach over to my nightstand, grab a condom from within the drawer and roll it on.

"Bra off," I demand. There is zero hesitation as she flicks the clasp in the front and her large breasts spill out of the cups.

Pulling one of her small pink nipples into my mouth, I suck before nipping with my teeth.

"Mike!" she cries out. I take that moment to push inside her, and although I just fucked her less than an hour ago, she's tight again. Her grip is fantastic around my cock.

"Hold your legs."

She grips behind her knees, opening up farther for me, and I lift her hips a little so I can watch her take my cock. It's fucking beautiful and I can't stop staring. The sight excites me enough that I can't hold back, so I brace myself above her and thrust hard. Her body jolts, breasts shaking with the impact, another sight that's so beautiful, I'll never forget it. I chase my orgasm down, my hips slamming into her repeatedly, until we both come, shaking and breathing hard. "God, that was even sexier than I thought it would be," I say.

After a moment of silence between us, she whispers, "I'm sorry I almost ruined the moment with the thing about the light."

"No worries, sweetheart." With a quick, soft kiss to her lips, I roll away to dispose of the condom. When I return to the bed, I slide up next to her and pull her against me.

"Tawney's a nasty bitch. She knew what would bother you, so she went for it, knowing I wasn't going to change my mind and ask her to stay and you to go. She wanted to make things difficult for us. M, you're the standard that every other woman in my life has been held to. It's why I never got married. There hasn't been another Summer for me."

"Mike . . ." she starts, but I hold my finger over her lips.

"Look around my house, M. How many pictures are there without you in them?" I don't wait for her answer, I tell her. "Maybe two. That should tell you a lot." Her eyes widen. "Please don't say a word, don't ruin my little fantasy here. Okay?" I plead. We stare into each other's eyes for a long time before she finally nods.

Scooter barks from the other side of the bed, startling both of us and making us laugh.

"Gotta take him out. Apparently he's tired of waiting." I place a quick peck on her lips before I stand. I pull a pair of dry basketball shorts from my drawer and tug them on, then I take Scooter out back to do his business.

After I let the dog out, I grab two beers and return to my room. Summer is seated with her back against the oak headboard of my bed, with the sheet pulled up under her arms.

She's holding a picture of her, Valerie, me, and my brother, Thomas, who was really little that year, in her hand, studying it with a faint smile on her face. I crawl up and sit next to her, passing her the beer. Her smile is brilliant when she turns to me.

"I've always wondered, what grown man has pictures of his childhood up around his bachelor pad?" she asks with a little giggle.

I take it from her and study it for a minute. It's from the first summer we were all together. Val and Summer were six or seven years old, I think. I was almost nine and Thomas was five. In the picture we're all sitting under the carport at my grandparents' house by the lake, wearing bathing suits while eating hunks of watermelon. Summer and Val are both laughing, and Thomas, with his toothless grin, is pretending to rub the watermelon in my hair, but I'm too busy smiling at the girls to notice my brother being an idiot.

There were a lot of those kinds of days. We spent the summers swimming and waterskiing in the lake during the day and playing freeze tag and hide-and-seek with other neighborhood kids in the evenings.

Grinning over at Summer, I tell her, "The kind of guy who decorates his bachelor pad with family pictures is the guy who knows what's important in life. You three have always mattered to me. The guys I hung out with in school all got married and drifted away. I see them from time to time and we enjoy ourselves. It's cool, but it's nothing like what we all had. Even Thomas is still one of my best friends despite the four-year age gap. Most people don't have memories like we have together, and I'm just the kind of guy who understands and appreciates it. This picture is one of my favorites."

"Is that why it's next to your bed?"

"Yeah." I take a swig of my beer and set it down on the nightstand before passing the picture back to her.

"Why does it look like Scooter chewed on the corner of the photo?"

"Scooter never chewed on the corner. It's because I carried it in my pocket while I was deployed."

She turns to me, her eyes wide. "You carried this picture with you?"

"My first platoon sergeant used to ask us to remember who we were fighting for when we'd go out on a mission. He wanted us to focus on one person or a small group of people, like a wife and kids. He felt that it helped to keep us focused. It's easy to lose sight of the reasons you signed up in the first place, when you see the shit we had to see and do practically every day. He asked us every single time to remember who we were fighting for, so I made it a point to always have a physical reminder on me. You guys were it."

"We're what you were fighting for?" Her voice is soft as she sets the picture and beer down and curls into me.

"Yeah." I wrap my arms around her and think about all the nights I wasn't sure I was going to make it out alive. Too many of those to count. The day I signed all my retirement paperwork and walked out the door as a civilian, I finally took a deep breath and thanked God I'd made it home in one piece. Too many of the guys I served with didn't.

"You tired?" she asks.

"Yeah, a little, but I'm afraid to go to sleep. I've waited a long time to get to this place with you. I don't want to waste a minute."

She kisses my bare chest and looks up at me.

"I told you, I'll be here all weekend. I'm tired. Let me use the restroom and turn off the lights so we can get at least a little sleep."

When she crawls back into bed, lifting my ridiculously fat hound up next to her, I spoon her, she spoons Scooter and we drift off with thoughts of what tomorrow could bring us.

4

Mike

I wake at the first sign of light coming through the blinds. Years of army regimen has left me with an internal clock set to ass-crack-of-dawn early, no matter what time I fell asleep the night before. All three of us are in the same position that we fell asleep in, which is a miracle considering Scooter usually gets up twice a night to find a new spot on the bed. It could have something to do with Summer curled around him. Even he's happier with her here and he's pretty damn happy. I still remember the day I got Scooter.

I found an injured feral kitten outside by my trash cans and took it to the local animal shelter. While I was filling out the paperwork to leave it there, I kept hearing this painful howling sound coming from the direction of the kennels. It was the most heartbreaking sound I've ever heard and it was bugging me, so once they took the kitten back to see their veterinarian, I asked the lady helping me if I could see the howler. The dog was down the second row of kennels toward the middle. His howling was loud, almost like he was crying.

"Can I pet him?" I asked the lady. I just wanted to soothe the poor guy.

"Well, he doesn't bite, so yeah. I'll warn you, though, he won't stop that sound no matter what we do."

When I stepped inside the caged area, his tail began to wag and the howling stopped for a second. I crouched down and put my hand out for him to smell. He gave me one quick bark in greeting before his cold nose sniffed and nudged my hand. The howling started again, but he didn't move or act like he wanted me to go away, so I reached over and stroked his soft fur. Naturally, I started talking to him over the painfully loud howling, explaining why I was there and how his howling made me sad. The howling died down to a slight whimper, so I continued talking, mostly nonsense. There was now some drooling and lots of wagging, but the awful sound was gone. Just as the kennel lady started to say something about it, my fingers caught on a rough patch in his fur. I leaned in closer and noticed what looked like raised stripe marks on the underside of his body.

"What are those?" I asked.

"His previous owner took a whip to him when he'd howl. We think he howls because he can now. Neighbors turned his owner in after they discovered him using a bullwhip on the dog one night. When he came to us, he had 13 open wounds and several other scars."

"How long have you had him here?"

"Over six months. No one wants a dog who makes that kind of racket, but he's sweet so we can't bear to put him to sleep."

When she said that, he plopped his fat body down and rolled over, exposing his whole stomach to me. As a grown man who's seen what I've seen, it takes a lot to make me cry, but the scars on his underside brought tears to my eyes. I stroked his underbelly gently for several minutes while he lay there quietly, his tongue lulling out the side of his mouth.

After 15 minutes, the lady said, "We'll be closing shortly,

and I need to get some paperwork done." I took that to mean she didn't want to stand there anymore while I petted him. Sadly, I said goodbye and walked away. As soon as we hit the entryway to the kennel, I could hear him start up again. The sound rang in my head even after I'd left him behind.

After a sleepless night, I went back and adopted him. He's been quiet ever since. He'll bark on occasion, but the howling never happens. Of course, they had him named something dumb, so I changed it to Scooter because when he walked, it looked like the middle of his body was scooting across the ground.

The first night I had him, my parents, brother, his current girlfriend—or his flavor of the week—and Summer came over for a cookout. As soon as Summer showed up, Scooter was glued to her. It was love at first sight. When she found out his history, she took extra care with him, and if I wasn't already in love with her then, that would have pushed me over the edge. From then on Scooter stayed on her heels or in her lap when she was at my house.

I head to the kitchen and start the coffee, then pull out the eggs and bacon and begin cooking. A few minutes into the task, I hear Scooter bark once so I look in the bedroom. He's sitting on the edge of the bed. He's too fat, too long and too short to jump down, so I scoop him up and lower him to the floor ready to take him outside.

"Why are you up so early?" Summer groans from the bed. Her blonde hair is wild from sleeping on it damp. The medusa hair doesn't diminish her beauty, though. Her golden skin and soft curves are laid out against my white sheets. Gorgeous. I lean down and kiss her quickly because Scooter's nudging me toward the door.

"Army life stayed with me. I'm up early every day. Wake up, sleepyhead. I want every minute I can get with you."

"Mike!" she squeals as I poke her side to tickle her before I dart out of the room to open the back door.

5

Summer

Damn that man! I'm not a morning person, never have been. I lie there, the smell of bacon hanging in the air while I hear him come and go from the backyard. Scooter trots in and stands by the bed, wagging and waiting for me to get up.

"Let's go to the lake house today. We can see Granny and Granddad and take the boat out for a little while," he yells from the kitchen.

"How about if we stay in bed all day. I'm tired," I whine.

"As tempting as that sounds, what I have in mind for the bed is not the same as you and you'll be sore if we stay." He rips the covers off me and scoops me out of bed before I have a chance to react.

"Mike!"

"Come on, let's eat and then get your medusa hair under control. Don't want you to scare Granny."

I do my best to scowl at him, but it doesn't work. I'm certain I look like I've been chewed up and spit back out, so I can't blame him for wanting me to get cleaned up.

After we eat and shower, Mike drives me by my place to

grab a swimsuit, and we head to his grandparents' house. Some of my best childhood memories are on this lake and with his family.

When we arrive, I get the usual hugs and hellos from his now frail grandparents, and we visit with them before heading to the dock. It takes a few minutes to get loaded up on the ski boat and out onto the water. The sun sits against the clear blue sky, causing little beads of sweat to appear along my hairline. It's early enough in the day that there aren't any clouds in the sky. Of course, by this afternoon, we'll have the usual thunderstorms, but for now it's the perfect Florida day. I prop myself in the same place I always do, in the front of the boat on one of the bench seats, with my legs stretched out in front of me. Mike gets behind the wheel and takes us out to the middle of the lake to anchor.

When he turns off the motor, he plugs his iPhone into the sound system and turns it up. I stand and stretch, enjoying the warm sun after being in the cool Colorado air for the last week. Florida lake water is dark and freaks most people out, but because I've been swimming here most of my life, that's not an issue for me.

Mike moves up to where I'm standing and wraps his strong arms around me. Smiling up at him, I note the contemplation in his eyes and wonder what's on his mind. Before I can ask, he dips down to kiss me. It's sweet and slow. Different than any kiss we've had so far. A few started out that way, but always morphed into way more. Not this time though.

"Give me your sunglasses," he says as he takes his own off.

"Why? It's bright out here."

He smiles at me but doesn't answer, so like an idiot I take them off and pass them to him. He lays both sets on the seat where I was previously sitting, quickly scoops me up, and the next thing I know, we're flying over the bow of the boat and through the air toward the water. The weather may be warm, but because it's spring-fed water, the lake is cold out here in the middle, and I was hoping to work my way in slowly. I cringe as we hit the water. I was right . . . it's cold. I shoot up, sputtering and cussing. "Mike, you're such a jerk! I wasn't warm enough yet to jump in this water!" I scold.

His laughter is loud as we tread water. "That was fun. Don't you think that was fun, M?"

I don't answer. Instead, I swim to the ladder and drag my now shivering butt out of the water and search for my towel.

"Come on. It was all in good fun. You knew we were getting in the water. I don't know why you're mad." He follows me up, watching me closely as I do my best to ignore him.

"I wasn't ready," I pout, obviously still a little grumpy from the early morning wake-up call. I spread my towel out and stretch out on the bench seat. He turns away, snatching his towel off the other seat and drying off, his back to me.

He stays quiet, the music playing is the only sound between us. Sitting down, he pulls his phone out. I'm not sure what he's doing on it, but he's typing and scrolling for what seems like forever. The more he stays quiet, the more time I have to realize I was being a bitch for no reason. He was only being playful. God, I hate feeling like such a jerk. It's a characteristic I get from my mom. I fight those quirks all the time, never wanting to be like the white-trash woman who sort of raised me. When the first few beats of a sexy song come through the speakers, I decide I'm going to make amends in a way he'll appreciate. I get up and make my way to him. When I'm finally standing directly in front of him, he lifts his face, but his eyes are shielded by the silver lenses of his aviator sunglasses.

Taking the phone from his hand and putting it back by the speaker, I crawl up in his lap, straddling his legs, and hold his cheeks with both my hands. "I'm sorry, I'm grumpy in the morning. I shouldn't have taken that out on you. You were just having fun." I hold my breath, waiting to see how he's going to react.

There is a long pause before he says, "Kiss me."

I lean in and press my lips to his as he wraps his arms around me, mashing my chest to his. Our kiss moves slowly, almost to the beat of the music, and my fingernails scrape along his scalp and down his neck, enough for him to feel it, but not enough to break the skin. He moans against my mouth, and I continue over his shoulders and arms. Our kiss goes deeper becoming frantic and heated. He grips my bottom and pulls me against him. His cock is hard, and I'm sure it's uncomfortable in those swim shorts. All I can think of is getting it inside me. I scoot back and stand as I tell him, "Take off your swimsuit." I then proceed to put on a brief but sexy show of shimmying my bottoms down extra slow while he shoves his down to the deck of the boat.

"Do you have a condom?"

"Fuck!" he groans, letting his head fall back and closing his eyes.

"Have you ever gone without one?" I ask, almost afraid of the answer. Relief rolls through me when he shakes his head no.

"I'm on the pill."

"You trust me?" he asks.

"You've never lied to me before."

He adjusts a little and I straddle him again, with one hand between us so I can line his cock up with my opening. I brace myself using his shoulder. As I slide down his shaft, he makes the strangest satisfied sound I've ever heard. "It's no wonder people don't want to use condoms. God, this is amazing."

He pulls the string behind my neck on my bikini top and the triangles flop down and hang, leaving my breasts bare. He cups them and pinches both, causing me to clench harder around him. I raise and lower on him over and over, grinding my hips on the down thrust, until he finally says, "I need more. I need harder. Get on your knees."

I climb off and set myself up so my knees are on the bench seat, spread the width of my shoulders, as I face the water. He grips my hips and slides in, each stroke in perfect sync with the sultry beat of the playlist running in the background. His hands move across the skin of my ass and back as he rocks into me until he finally gets around to my breasts. He pauses to tease me, tweaking my sensitive nipples. My reaction must turn him on because he changes pace and begins to pound, jolting my body forward each time and I moan. The harder he thrusts, the louder I get, until I'm calling his name on repeat and he's collapsing over me. I can feel the sweat from his torso along my back as he catches his breath. When he finally pulls out, I shudder. That's the first time someone has ever come in me without a barrier, and I love that it was Mike.

Using his T-shirt, he wipes us both clean. We slip back into our suits, and with his help, my bikini top is tied back in place.

"Want to jump in?" he asks.

I grin at him. "Yeah."

We spend the next couple of hours talking and floating with a couple of water noodles. My legs stay wrapped around his waist while his hands grip my thighs, holding me in place. It's relaxing and sweet and the only place I want to be.

"Do you remember Candy Sue?" I ask him, and he nods with a smile on his face.

I splash him a little bit when jealousy flares in my belly at his reaction.

"Hey! Hey! Hey! What was that for?" he chuckles a little as he asks.

"I was jealous as hell of her," I confess. "She was the first girl you ever ignored me for. When she was around, you couldn't see anything but her."

"That's because she was my first. All I could think about was the next time I'd get to screw her."

Rolling my eyes, I continue, "I didn't want to share you."

"Then why didn't you say anything?"

"Because you were dangerous. Handsome like my father and every girl in school wanted you. For a girl like me, whose father had to sleep with every available woman in town and left her mother without a glance back, someone like you looked like a bad idea. You had heartbreak written all over you, and if that happened between us, I'd lose the only real family I ever had—yours."

"Damn, M. I'd never have done anything to hurt you, even when I was thinking with my dick. I always wanted to be with you. It seemed you only liked the smart nerdy guys. Those poor dudes all thought they'd won the lottery when you turned your smile to them. But now I know they felt safe for you. There was no way any one of them would ever have cheated on a girl like you."

I nod, agreeing. I know why I did what I did. Hell, I still date that same kind of guy when I actually date.

"I'm not like your father. Look at my family, the history, the track record. My only influences are men that have been married to the same women forever and still seem to love them the way they always did. I know what your dad leaving did to you. I care enough about you not to do the same."

"Yeah, I get what you're saying, but I have trust issues, and you may have been raised by good influences in the relationship department, but you still date women like Tawney."

He opens his mouth to defend himself, and I kiss him to stop the words. "I don't want to talk about it anymore. I want to enjoy our time together. I'm sorry I brought it up. I was going in a different direction with this conversation than we took, so let's just let it go."

He kisses me back instead of saying anything else. "Come on, we need to get back to my place to let Scooter out," he says.

We swim back to the boat and head for his grandparents' home, a little quieter than when we started the day.

6

Mike

Twice during the night, I wake Summer to make love to her. I want her to see what's in my heart, and I don't know how else to show it. I'm gentle and take my time to kiss and stroke every inch of the incredibly soft skin on her body. It doesn't seem like I can get enough of her, and I'm afraid that tomorrow will bring forth the end of my dream. Tawney being here the night we got home didn't help my odds, that's for sure, but there's more to it than that. Summer is still scared of being left behind with a broken heart. I'd love to track her dad down and beat his old wrinkled ass for making her feel the way she does, but that wouldn't solve anything. The damage has already been done.

I leave the bed so I can start the coffee and take Scooter out. Of course, he's quiet and comfortable, snuggled up to Summer and I almost hate to wake him, but I want every minute I can get with her when she wakes up.

When I return to the bed, she's rolled to her back with one arm bent above her head, one breast uncovered. She's still asleep, but I can't pass up the opportunity to taste her, so I dip my head close and suck the sweet pink tip into my mouth.

When I flick it with my tongue, a little moan slips from her, and I smile before I repeat the process. This time her hand comes down and her nails dig into my scalp, holding me there against her. I continue to tease her until her eyes open. A little smile plays on her lips, and I pull the other side of the sheet down to move my attention to the other breast.

"Yes," she moans and closes her eyes again.

I kiss a line down over her rib cage, across her belly and down to her sex. She squirms and opens her legs wide for me. After I spread the lips of her sex with my fingers, I swipe at her most tender of places as gently as I can with my tongue. I know she's probably sore. We've had a lot of sex this weekend. I have to be careful that my morning stubble doesn't abrade her skin. I dip my tongue inside, enjoying the taste of her. When she squirms, obviously impatient, I glance up to find her watching me with hooded eyes. My palms slide up the inside of her thighs, holding them open, and I focus my effort directly on her clit. Our gazes remain locked as I increase the flicker speed of my tongue until she can't take it anymore. When her clit swells, I pull it between my lips and gently bite down on it. Her whole body arches off the bed and she cries out my name. I close my eyes and slow my pace to drain every last drop from her sweet pussy. No woman I've ever been with has tasted this good.

I drag myself up and lie next to her, hard as a rock but trying to talk myself down. I don't want her to reciprocate. Well, I do, but I don't. I want to have given her something she didn't have to repay. I pull her against me, and she rests with her head on my chest and one arm over my stomach.

"Thank you," she says, before she kisses the bare skin near my nipple.

"Anything for you, M."

"I can't believe you still call me that."

I turn just enough so she can look up and see my eyes.

"When was the last time you ate M&M's?" I ask, knowing the answer.

She smacks my gut and laughs.

"I rest my case. Yesterday, at my Granny's house, you ate half the jar she keeps there for your visits. When was the time before that?"

She pokes me in the side and I squirm. I hate being tickled, even if it's only a little.

"The flight home. See, it's a well-earned nickname. That first summer we hung out together, you and Val made me walk you to the convenience store every day so she could get jelly-beans and you could get M&M's. I've never seen an obsession like you two had with that candy."

"God, you've known me too long. I have no secrets from you." She scoots up to kiss me and as she's pulling away, her phone rings.

"I'll be right back," she tells me and goes in search of the device.

"Hello," she answers.

"Yeah, I'm in Tampa. With a friend. Why?"

"What!" she yells, and I can hear the excitement in her voice. "Oh my gosh! Are you serious?"

There's a pause, followed by a frustrated sigh, and then I can hear the creak of the wood on the kitchen floor as she begins to pace back and forth.

"Yeah, can you make the flight midafternoon? I have to go home and get clean clothes. I still haven't unpacked from Colorado."

My heart rate picks up, and the dread that sat in my gut all night long works its way up my throat.

"Okay, text me the details. Thanks, Mick!"

I hear a loud exhale, and then she appears in the doorway. I climb out of bed because I know that phone call ended my weekend earlier than I expected. I'm pulling on a T-shirt and slipping on a pair of flip-flops as she watches me from the doorway.

"That was Mick, my agent. Connie Dunkin—the director I've been hoping to work with—had to fire an actress yesterday for using drugs on the set, and she has asked for me to take the actress's place. I have to fly to Maine this afternoon if I want the part. They need me to join the cast now."

"Is it a lead?" I ask, wishing it is so I can justify her leaving in my head.

"No, but it's not a role as an extra. The fact that she asked for me is huge. I have to take this. At my age, I have no idea how many chances I'll get, so I need to take any that are thrown my way. Please don't be mad."

I sit on the edge of the bed and summon her over with my hand. When she steps between my legs, I can see the tension in her shoulders and the worry in her eyes.

"What's next after this, M?"

"I've got a couple of auditions in LA, followed by a maga-zine shoot in France, and then I come back to start working that movie *Shadow Key* in Key West. I'll be in and out for the next year with different projects."

"How are we going to make this work?" I ask, but I already know the answer.

Tears fill her eyes. "I can't do long-distance, Mike. I know my limits and I can't do it. I trust you more than I trust most anyone, but not enough to be away for most of a year. It's too much to ask when you have women like Tawney naked in your room when you return home."

"That never happens and you know it."

"You get what I mean. I'll always worry that you're tired of waiting. I'll always think the worst. It's programmed in me. I don't think I can do it."

She's full-on crying now, and I can't stand it. I'd like to punch a few doors and yell the walls down, but I'm too practical for that. It won't do any good. If I thought it would make a difference, I'd fight for her, but I've known her long enough to know it won't change a thing.

I pull her in tight against me and whisper, "I understand. Don't cry, it's gonna be okay. I'll still be here for you . . . always. If you change your mind, you can call me. If you don't change your mind, you can call me. Nothing has to change." With every word my heart breaks, with every lie it gets harder to breathe, but I love her enough to let her go. Hell, I've gone this long without her, I know I can do it. The difference is now I know for certain what I've been missing. We fit in a way neither of us ever have before with anyone else. But I can't force it, won't pressure her.

With a quick kiss to the top of her hair, I release her and walk toward the door. "Get your stuff together, and I'll let Scooter out before I take you home." I can't look at her because I don't want her to see me cry. I'm too proud for that. It's bad enough that I'm crying at all, but to allow her to see that . . . Nope. Not going to happen.

7

Summer

I pack my stuff at warp speed. I'll have minimal time once I get home to shower, change and repack. This is an opportunity I can't pass up because it'll likely lead to other opportunities I can grab hold of.

My modeling and acting career all started when my friend whom I was waiting tables with, Simone, wrote a romance novel. She asked me to be on the cover so I did it. I'd always wanted to be a model or an actress, but couldn't seem to land anything when I was younger. I had a few callbacks, did a commercial a long time ago, but nothing went anywhere. My mom got cancer and I stopped in order to take care of her, but it didn't matter. I was always too short, too curvy, too blonde, too tan. When I decided to stick my toe in the water and try again after she recovered, I was told I was too old. I figured nothing would ever happen, so I gave up. I did that photoshoot for Simone's book, and a couple of the extra pictures that were taken for stock photos sold, but that was it.

Simone's book made the best seller list, and she ended up doing pretty well and needed an assistant. That assistant took the book—with me on the cover—on a flight and got seated next to Phil Harmon, one of the biggest directors in Hollywood. He inquired about the cover model, got my information and had me audition for him. The next thing I knew, my agent was telling me that Mr. Harmon would like me for a supporting role in his next movie. Things sort of took off from there. I've done a few magazine shoots and lined up some movie parts. It's enough to pay my bills. So, although I don't think it will last forever, I'm enjoying living the dream for now, and I'll continue to do so until my good fortune stops.

When my packing is complete, I drag my suitcase out of Mike's room with a quick glance back at his bed. This weekend is one I'll never forget, and I'm not sure how I'll move on from it, but just like every other relationship in my life I *will* move on from it. I *will* forget what it's like to be held and loved. I'll also forget what it's like to sleep soundly because you know the man with his arms around you will never let any harm come to you. Yes, I *will* forget all of that.

Mike's pouring coffee into two travel mugs as I bend down and scratch Scooter's head, letting him lick my cheek at the same time.

"Goodbye, Scooter-boy. I'll see you again soon," I say to him.

Mike passes me the two coffees and grabs my suitcase, pulling it to the door.

As soon as the door closes, Scooter begins to howl so loud I know the neighbors are going to freak out. I turn wide eyes to Mike, and he rests his head on the doorjamb like this is something he doesn't want to deal with now.

"Go on to the car, let me see if I can quiet him," he tells me, slipping back inside for a couple of minutes until the howling finally dies down. I could hear it all the way in the truck, it was so loud. Mike loads up my suitcase and takes me home in silence.

When we arrive, he walks me to the door, placing my suitcase inside. Then he threads his fingers into the hair on both sides of my head and leans his forehead against mine as his eyes close.

"Thank you for this weekend, and thank you for the last 34 years. I'm here for you just like I've always have been, okay?" His voice is shaky. If he breaks down, I'll lose it. I've only seen it happen once before, when a friend of ours from school was killed in a car accident right after he graduated.

"Okay," I tell him, afraid to say more. How can I love someone this much and still walk away? How is that possible? I'll probably spend the rest of my life sorry I said no to trying to make this work.

"Call me when you're in town long enough for dinner. Mom and Dad are going to want to see you." His eyes are sad, but he's doing his best not to let it show.

"Yes, I'll call like I always do."

After one final mind-bending, panty-melting kiss, he turns and strides back to his truck. I'm certain it's actual heartbreak that's causing the intense pain in my chest, and I can't believe I'm letting him walk away. The tears now silently gliding down my face tell me a truth I'm not ready to listen to. I am, without a doubt, in love with Michael Wade. I only wish I was strong enough to take the risk of being in a relationship with a man as amazing as he is.

8

Mike

One year later . . .

The Florida sun warms my skin as I relax. Working for Security Six isn't usually stressful for me, but our last job was hostage rescue in South America. It took its toll and I'm in need of the couple weeks of rest and relaxation I'm currently enjoying alone. The sound of the waves breaking in the background have lulled me into a comfortable trance. The best part about being back in the Sunshine State is the beach. I've always been a sucker for the sun and sand that surrounds me here.

The ringing of my phone snaps me out of the zone, and I lift my sunglasses up to glance at the caller ID. *Summer Arden* the screen reads. I smile to myself.

As soon as I hit the button to connect I ask, "M, how are you?"

"Mike . . ." Her voice breaks like she's crying, and all my senses go on high alert. Summer is one of the most positive, upbeat people I know, so if she sounds like this, there's a problem.

"What's wrong?" I ask, unable to hide the worry.

She sniffles and I fight the instinct to yell at her to tell me what's going on. "Come on, M. You have to say something."

"I'm in Key West filming Shadow Key and someone broke into my hotel room while we were out filming this morning and left . . . stuff in my bed. God, Mike, I'm so scared. I know you're finally getting some time off, but I didn't know who else to call. I need you."

"You're still at the Marriot?" I ask, already standing and gathering my belongings as I wait for her to answer.

"Yeah. I've got a few more days here. The weather messed up filming two of the days, so we had to add time. I'm so sorry. I know how little time you get off."

"Don't say another word, M. I've always told you that if you need me I'm there. Text me your address. Is there more to this story that you aren't telling me? It's not like you to get spooked like this."

"Yes, but we'll talk about it when you get here. I'll pay your expenses."

"You aren't paying for shit. Text me the address. I'm sending someone over there to sit with you until I can get there. I'll text you his picture and name. Don't open your door for anyone else."

"I'm not in my room. I'm with Maggie, one of the other actresses, in her room. I can't go back in there."

When she sniffles and whimpers a little, I wish I had a jet I could jump in to make the trip faster. Six and a half hours is too long to worry. Fuck!

"Don't let anyone into that room except you two. Don't order room service until I have someone with you. That door stays locked and you stay put."

"We have to shoot again this afternoon. I don't have as many scenes as Maggie but I still need to be there the whole time."

"You can go to the set once I get someone with you. I'm

hanging up to call my friend. I'll text you what you need. Just hold tight, sweetheart."

"Okay, I will. Thanks, Mike."

"You're welcome. Gotta go, hon."

"Bye," she says softly and hangs up.

Damn it! I locate Hudson McCormick's number—my buddy who works at Security Six with me—and dial quickly as I swing into my jeep and throw it in gear, switching to my Bluetooth.

"Hudson," a deep voice answers.

"It's Mike Wade. Gotta call in a marker. You still in the Keys?"

"Yeah, I was leaving today for the Bahamas but I can hold off. What's up?"

"I don't know. My sister's best friend is an actress. She's in Key West filming a movie. Some freak broke into her room. There's more to the story, but I didn't get all the particulars. She's scared and I'm in St. Pete. It'll take me six and a half hours to get there without traffic. Any chance you can go play bodyguard until I arrive? She has to shoot later today, and I don't want her going to the set without protection. I'm almost home and can be back out the door in about 10 minutes."

"Anything, man. You know that. Text me the address. I'll send you a picture of me right now. Tell her not to open that door for anyone else. I'm in Marathon which is about an hour from Key West and can leave now."

"Thanks, man. Call me when you get there and figure out what the hell is going on. I didn't want to waste time with details until I had her covered."

"You got it. See you soon."

I hang up and spend the next several minutes calling around to find someone to look after Scooter. Thank God for my neighbor.

Summer. Her name rolls over and over in my head and my

gut clenches. I haven't seen her much since our weekend spent between the sheets last year, but that doesn't mean I want her less. The timing wasn't right for us to take things further, but it's not because I didn't want it. The end of our amazing weekend is the only heartbreak I remember suffering since high school. Of course, I'll never tell her that. Our friendship was more important in the end than anything else—or that's what I keep telling myself. More than anything, I haven't wanted the awkwardness of unrequited love to take away what little time I do get with her.

AN HOUR AND A HALF LATER, my phone rings with Hudson's number on the caller ID and I answer.

"Hey, you got her?" I ask, impatient to know she's okay.

"Yeah, I'm with her and she's fine, but you're not gonna like this situation. This isn't the first time she's had an incident. This is number 10 and things seem to be escalating."

"Ten?" I shout. "Same guy? What do you mean 'escalating'?"

"Dude did a cum dump on her bed and used her lipstick to leave a little note on the headboard."

"What in the ever-loving fuck?" I growl, ready to punch the shit out of something. No wonder she called me freaked out. "What did the note on the headboard say?"

"You're mine."

I drop a string of cuss words. "Don't leave her side until I get there."

"No problem, relax, you know she'll be fine with me. Besides, it's not a hardship. You didn't tell me she was smokin'."

"Back the fuck off, dude," I growl, knowing I'd go to blows with my friend if he tried to take it there with her.

He laughs long and hard. "Sister's best friend, my ass," he says between guffaws.

"Screw you. Don't worry about anything except keeping her safe. I'll be there as soon as I can." I disconnect without a goodbye, his laughter coming through the line as I do. *Bastard.*

9

Summer

It was all I could do not to call Mike each time I received something that would send chills down my spine from this stalker, but the mess in my bed ended that effort. There's no one that makes me feel as safe as Mike Wade, and I'm lucky enough that he was on a break from work. Since he retired from the Army Special Forces, he's been part of a private security team in Tampa. Security, personal protection, and information gathering seem to be Mike's main duties and he's been on an assignment out of the country for three weeks. We had dinner with his family right before he left, and he texted me yesterday to let me know he was home.

I probably should have called Mike when this all started, but I didn't want to overreact. At age 43, I didn't expect to have a career in acting and modeling—that just seems ridiculous—and even more so, I didn't expect to have a crazed stalker. But apparently, I do.

For the past few weeks, I've been getting emails and handwritten notes with ostentatious bouquets of flowers from a person named C. With the first bouquet, I was flattered that someone would send me flowers. When the second delivery came, I blew it off because another actress I was working with said it was normal. I'm sure it's more common with the younger actresses and models, but after her assurances that this happens all the time I tried to forget about it. Considering the notes were always signed C, I wasn't certain it was a man until today when I found the "present" he left me. It wasn't so freaky when the gifts were coming to the door. I felt like there was a barrier between me and whoever was doing this—a false sense of safety, I guess. Today's mess feels like a violation of my space and my privacy and is so disgusting it makes me want to puke. What kind of person does something like this?

The guy Mike sent over here to watch out for me is no joke. Hudson has muscles on top of muscles and looks like he might even be able to break Mike in half. Mike is no slouch in the big badass guy department, but Hudson is a whole other level of tough guy. Silent and deadly without a doubt. He's also younger than Mike and me by almost 10 years if I had to take a guess. The muscled beast is a handsome devil, that's for sure, and I bet he's lethal when he needs to be.

Tired of sitting in silence while Maggie's in the corner typing on her laptop, I turn to Hudson. "You work for the same company as Mike?" I ask.

He nods. "Freelance for now."

I figured he was, but I needed somewhere to start the conversation with him. The silence is driving me nuts.

"Do you live in the Keys year-round? And don't you dare give me a one-word answer. The quiet in here is making me batty."

He cracks an unexpected boyish grin and I relax slightly.

"No, I inherited my grandparents' house in Marathon when they died. I come down here for R and R. Wade happened to catch me before I took off for the Bahamas."

"I'm sorry this messed up your trip," I tell him, feeling bad for taking away from his off time with my situation.

"I'm not. I can leave later tonight or tomorrow. No big deal."

"Got a girlfriend or a wife or something?"

"Nope. You looking to apply for the position?" He grins again, and if I hadn't grown up with the Wade boys and their flirty smartass ways, I'd be surprised by his comment. But one thing you learn around a bunch of smartasses is how to throw them off balance with a response they don't anticipate.

"Actually yes. I've been sitting over here thinking about what our kids would look like and if you'd like my cat or if we'd have to get a dog. How do you feel about cats? Butterball is a sweet cat, although she's fat and likes to sleep on top of the head of my lovers. She really is a great cat." I feign sincerity. "She's only interrupted sex a few times so I can feed her. It wasn't too bad until she clawed the last guy's ass in the middle of doing the business."

The smirk slips from his lips as I stare at him, straight-faced, waiting for his response.

"I. . . I . . . I . . ." he stammers.

I bust out laughing so loud the whole floor can probably hear me. Maggie glances up from her computer and glares at me. She's too uptight; I should be the one with a bad attitude here. She didn't come back to find some guy's baby-batter all over her sheets.

"I'm just fucking with you, solider. Stand down. I'm tired of sitting here in silence, so I'm trying to find things to make you talk. One-word answers don't cut it. I thought if you had a girlfriend, you might have something to talk about."

"Nah, I don't have a girl. With my line of work, it's hard to keep someone in my life steady. It's been my experience that women like to be able to plan dates and trips and want to know where you are when you're not with them. There are too many times when we're put on a job in the morning and it's wheels up by lunchtime, with no certain end date. It's hard to have and plan a life—much less take care of a girlfriend or wife—with that kind of schedule."

"You could do something else for a living, I'm sure." I state the obvious.

"Nah, I'm pretty happy with my life. If you tried to put me behind a desk, I'd wither and die. Besides, I don't have a problem finding companionship." He grins again.

I blush a little because I'm certain he doesn't have that problem, and I get a brief mental picture of him having "companionship" with someone. After that I remain quiet and wait.

A couple of hours later Maggie's phone alarm goes off, and I put down the magazine I've been mindlessly flipping through. It's time to return to the set.

"Ready?" she asks.

I nod, standing to stretch and slip on my sandals. Hudson stands in front of the door waiting for Maggie to grab her bag.

"How did you plan to get to the location?" he asks.

"The producer is sending a car for us. We're supposed to meet him outside by the valet stand," Maggie answers.

"Summer can't stand out in the open like that. We'll stand inside until you see the car, then we'll go out together."

"I doubt she needs *that* kind of protection," Maggie scoffs, and I kind of agree with her. I've never been approached before. Everything has always come to my hotel room or home through a delivery person. Well . . . until today.

Hudson doesn't bend. "Wade put me in charge of keeping Summer safe until he gets here. I don't fu—screw around."

"This is kind of inconvenient," Maggie tells him, tapping her toe, perturbed.

Hudson's head tilts to the side like he's sizing her up. "I realize not being able to stand outside and sweat your ass off is inconvenient, but we're talking the safety of your friend."

"No one has ever even approached her," she complains.

I shake my head. So glad my safety is a concern of hers.

"Not that you know of. I guarantee he's had some kind of contact with her; she just didn't realize who it was. Guys that do shit like this are usually smart enough not to break into a hotel room and leave a full DNA sample behind, but once they get sloppy like this, you can be sure shit's about to get ugly. So, if it's too big of a bother"—the sarcasm is dripping from his voice—

"to keep your friend safe, you can go out and wait for the car outside. Ms. Arden will remain with me inside until I can escort her straight to the vehicle."

Maggie huffs and stomps outside without another word. Why is she so bent out of shape? It doesn't seem like that big of a deal to wait inside the doors until the car arrives.

"Your friend's kind of a bitch, babe," he remarks.

"She's another actress. We haven't spent much time together. She's a new friend, maybe not even that, with her blatant disregard for my safety. Even if I think you're going a little overboard."

Hudson doesn't say anything. His eyes scan the crowd in the lobby, the elevator area, the front desk and the people coming and going. I don't think anyone questionable could make it into this area without him spotting them. With the number of people in this place, I'm thankful he's here because, for the first time since this started, I'm feeling nervous and vulnerable. This whole thing seems surreal.

"Thank you for postponing your trip to be here. I appreciate it. I know you're doing this for Mike, but I just wanted you to know I'm grateful."

"No problem." A man of few words. I smile to myself as we wait.

10

Mike

I pull into the Key West hotel parking lot, park and wipe my palms on my shorts before I climb out of the vehicle. The only time I've ever been this impatient is when my sister came home from deployment to find out her husband left her, also taking my niece with him. Because of a layover in Dallas, it took me eight hours to get to my distraught sister in Colorado. I was like a caged, agitated lion and the feeling is just as strong now.

Hudson texted 20 minutes ago and said he and Summer were back at the hotel after filming. He was standing guard outside room 233—her new room—because she was showering and getting dressed. There were no incidents while she was on set, and her room was fine when they returned, which could be because I had the hotel staff put her in a room under my name and credit card. I don't want to make it too easy for anyone who's targeting her.

Leaving the elevator, I turn left and spot Hudson leaning against the wall, eyes on me. His stance is casual. He's in his cargo shorts and T-shirt like he's waiting on a friend, not guarding Summer's life.

"Hey, man. Thanks for helping me out. How is she?"

"She's shaken up, but better since we came back to no issues with her new room."

"Do you have any thoughts on this? Did she say anything more that gave you any ideas of what this might be about?"

"No, she had no idea. But it's not hard to understand why she's a target. She's smokin' hot and sweet as pie. Past that, the reason is nothing other than there are sick fucks out there who get off on scaring people like her. Police collected the evidence and took her statement. Unless this dude is on one of the video cameras or his DNA is already in the system, they won't be able to do much and she's freaked."

"That's part of the reason I wanted you here, to let her know someone has her back. You can cut out now. I'll knock and let her know I'm here."

After we shake hands, Hudson turns on his heel and saunters toward the elevator as I knock on the door. "M, it's me, let me in." After a couple of seconds, I can hear the locks flip, and then the door is open and she's in my arms. This is déjà vu, my sister did the same thing when I got to Colorado. Keeping my arms tight around her, I back her into her room and lock the door behind us. Muffled sobs are absorbed by my chest as I continue to hold her. My heart aches at the sadness and fear I know she's feeling, and I'll do anything to take that away.

"M, look at me, sweetheart." Her sniffles are quieter when she leans back. The slightly upturned nose that I think is so damn cute is red, along with her eyes, setting off the sapphire color so it shines brighter.

"I'm so sc-sc-scared," she sobs and drops her head to my chest again.

"I know, but you don't have to be. I won't let anyone hurt you."

"I know you have to go back to work soon. What will I do then?"

"I don't know, but I won't leave you unprotected. Trust me, please."

"Okay." Her acceptance is quiet.

"For tonight, we're eating here in the room until I get more information and decide what to do. I don't want any extra exposure for you."

THE REST of the evening is spent catching up. It's only been a few weeks since we saw each other but there's still plenty to talk about. When it's time for bed, I reach into the closet and grab a pillow and blanket with the intention of sleeping on the couch in the suite portion of the room. I don't want to sleep that far from her, but we've been careful to keep our relationship "friends only" since our sinful weekend.

"Put that away, Michael Wade, and get your butt in here," Summer barks from the doorway to her room. When I turn to her, I scan her from head to toe. My midnight angel is wearing an oversized white T-shirt that looks oddly familiar with the name of a Tampa brewery stitched in blue. Her shiny blonde hair hangs loose past her shoulders. Her tanned, toned arms and legs are visible and tempting me in a way I shouldn't even be thinking about right now.

"Is that my T-shirt?" I ask, already knowing the answer but wanting to hear her admit it.

"Yeah." She gives me a shy smile.

"It's been missing for a while."

"I accidently took it with me when I left last year, but couldn't bring myself to give it back to you. Sorry." Her expression is anything but repentant.

"You really want me to share the bed with you?" I can't help but smile at her. I wasn't about to assume I was sleeping in the bed with her. She nods so I shove the stuff back on the shelf in the closet and follow her retreating form into the dark room. I didn't realize it was possible to be that gorgeous in a freaking T-shirt, but it obviously is. I'm glad she kept it.

I lie down on my back and pull the blanket up to my waist. I hear her gulp the water that was sitting on the nightstand, and then I feel the bed depress as she climbs in. She doesn't bother acting shy or unfamiliar, instead she slides all the way over with her back along my side. I learned when we were together the last time that she likes the spoon position to sleep in, so I roll slightly and wrap an arm around her waist. The scent of her shampoo reminds me of the jasmine trellis in my parents' backyard. I'm not much for floral scents, but that's one I love.

I kiss the top of her hair and hold her tight against me. "You're gonna be okay. I'd give my own life before I let something happen to yours."

"Don't say that. If something happens to you because of me, I'll never forgive myself."

"There are things you don't know about me that I can't tell you because they're classified, but please know that some pansy-ass stalker won't best me. You couldn't have called a better person for this job."

"I've always felt safe with you, even when we were kids. It's why I called you first." She rolls in my arms to face me, and I curse myself for not leaving a light on so I could see her face better. The glow from the night-light I left on for her isn't enough. She's visible but shadowed some, and I feel the heat from her breath because her lips are so close to mine right now. I have a hundred ideas of what I'd like to do to those lips, but I know this isn't the time. I just need to remind my cock of that fact, because it slowly stiffens as her hand moves along the bare skin of my chest and down my abs. Fuck! If she reaches the waistline of my boxer briefs, she's going to know I have zero control with her. Her simple touch has me so hard in seconds that the head of my dick is peeking out of the waistband.

She's always done this to me, though. When we were in high school, Summer stood at the forefront of all of my jacking-off fantasies. You'd think an absolute knockout like her would be dating the captain of the football or basketball team, but she never did. I asked my sister about it once and she said, "I have no idea. She just likes guys with brains, I guess."

I was second in my class in academics, captain of the football team and captain of the mathletes, so I should've fit the bill—but she never looked at me that way. I always assumed it had to do with my football status. I just didn't know why.

"Make love to me, Mike," she quietly requests.

"Summer . . ." I'm not sure what to finish that sentence with. *Yes, please?* Or *No, because when you walk away again it will destroy me?* There's no good answer for that request.

"Please. I need you closer. I need the distraction, and you're the best kind."

My heart squeezes a little. I don't want to be her distraction. I don't want to be her in-the-moment guy. I want to be her twenty-four seven partner and best friend. I want to marry this woman and have 10 kids. Okay, so maybe not 10, we are a little old for that dream, but at least one. If she had any idea, though, of what I feel for her, she'd jump out of this bed and run like hell, so I keep quiet.

Instead of saying anything that might end what's about to happen, selfishly I grab her hand and move it over the bulge in my boxers. She squeezes and strokes me over the fabric and I stifle a moan.

I'm unable to hold back, so I slip my hand under her T-shirt, and when my fingers connect with her smooth, cool skin, I can't remain quiet any longer. I could spend hours touching her skin and stroking the contours of her body. I grip her hair with my other hand and hold her in place so I can plunder her mouth. When I finally end the kiss, it's with a slight nip to her lower lip. I'm careful not to leave a mark that would cause issues with her filming tomorrow, though. Quickly, I shift her to her back and trail soft kisses with little tongue strokes down the column of her throat as her body squirms beneath me. I continue down over her chest to tease the hardened peaks of her breasts through the fabric of the T-shirt, loving her reaction.

"Mike," she pants, and I can't help but smile. I push her shirt up to expose the tanned bronze section of her stomach and press kisses down the length and over her belly button. Hooking my fingers in the side of her tiny panties, I tug them down her legs. With a gentle grip on her knees, I lift and open, spreading her legs wide and moving my face in close. Summer has the most beautiful natural musk. It's light and sweet, like her, and I've dreamt of it since the last time my face was buried here.

I open her up with my fingers and inhale, groaning as I immerse myself in her. Then I take my time exploring each fold with my tongue, lapping at her with patience I don't feel. Summer enjoys the slow build, so I'm making sure she gets that. Her body squirms and bucks as she gets closer to explosion. Slipping two fingers inside her tight, hot channel, I know she's ready for me to take her over the edge. I concentrate on the little pleasure bud at her center, sucking and stroking, simultaneously working her fast and hard with my fingers until her knees close around my head, and she bucks her hips upward, screaming out my name. I can't help my smug smile. That was the exact reaction I was working for. As she comes down, I slip my fingers out of her and into my mouth for one last taste. I groan and crawl up so we are face-to-face. Now I have her leg hiked up higher so she's open as my cock rests against the wet heat between her legs. When I press my lips to hers, I feel her grin.

"Did you go to school for that? I don't think anyone knows how to go down on a woman as well as you do."

"I haven't been with anyone since you, M," I tell her, waiting for her reaction, praying for the same response. I hold my breath as she tortures me by making me wait.

"After a year? You haven't? You've always been very active. I find it hard to believe." Her eyes never leave mine.

"After you . . ." I pause, trying to find a way to tell her without spooking her. "No one fits me like you do. We make sense in so many ways, and after I had the real thing, hooking up for the hell of it lost its appeal. I swear I haven't been with anyone else."

"You really feel that way?" she asks, so hesitant and unsure it hurts my heart a little.

"God, M, you have no clue, do you? You aren't the mistress or the one-night stand. You aren't the sometimes-girl or the as-needed lay. If you'd let me, I'd marry you tomorrow. I've been half in love with you since we were kids, and I think I fell the rest of the way when we spent that weekend together. We fit Summer, and once you've had that, no one else comes close."

"Mike . . ." she whispers as tears pool in her eyes and a small smile forms on her lips. "I've never had that."

"You've always had that, with me. You just didn't want to face it. Have you been with anyone else?" I keep pushing because I want to bypass the condoms. We did last time, but I won't unless she hasn't been with anyone else.

"No, and I'm still on birth control. Make love to me, Mike."

I don't wait another second as I shift my hips and nudge her opening. Her pussy fits me like a glove and my muscles quiver with restraint. My instinct is animalistic, pushing me to pound into her until she screams my name and I own her. I want it loud enough that any other man who's been sniffing around her can hear and know. That any other man who has even been considering approaching her hears it and runs. She's mine and I'm ready to prove it to the world. But I fight my sexual beast, wanting her to feel the tenderness I have for her. It's important that she knows what's in my heart. I need her to know I've wanted this, wanted her, all of her, for as long as I can remember.

My hips start slow, pumping in and out of her as my mouth takes hers in a slow sensual kiss. When I break the kiss, I prop up on my elbows so I can watch as her body accepts mine with each stroke. The vision is erotic as hell, and the thought of videotaping it so I can replay it for personal use when we're apart is strong.

As her breathing increases and her eyes roll back in her head, I thrust harder, forcing sweat to slide down between my shoulder blades. Her pussy flutters and grips me tighter, and I work harder, taking her all the way. For the first time in my life, I come at the same time as my partner and my brain scrambles on overload. I drop my head into the pillow and kiss her exposed shoulder and neck.

"I love you, M. Always have." I hold my breath, thinking maybe I should have kept my mouth shut. Panic sets in so I kiss her, taking away the chance for her to reject me or say something I don't want to hear.

When I pull away, I climb out of bed. "Come on, let's get cleaned up so we can get some sleep. I want to be alert tomorrow so I don't miss anything." She's watching me carefully until she finally nods. I'm just praying she doesn't say something that will break my heart tonight.

11

Summer

What do I do? Mike Wade just told me he loves me. My whole life I've avoided men like him. Sexy, beautiful, popular, intelligent, athletic . . . *everything*. I learned from my mom never to fall in love with a man as amazing as Mike. My father was one of those guys. My parents met in high school and supposedly fell in love. He found out Mom was pregnant and then proceeded to sleep with everyone but her for the next year. Then he finally left and I only saw him once.

I didn't believe my mom when she said he didn't want me, so I tracked him down when I got my driver's license at 16. He was an even bigger bastard than she'd said. He's the best-looking man his age I've ever seen. Blond hair, blue eyes and tan skin. I was his female spitting image, he couldn't deny I was his if he tried.

When I introduced myself, he asked, "What are you doing here?" He didn't want to know anything about me, wasn't even curious about me in the slightest.

"I wanted to meet you," I answered, obviously intimidated.

"Your mother sent you for more child support. I told her the last time, that's all I'm giving."

"You send child support?" I asked, shocked. I didn't know there was any contact at all, much less money coming in for me. Mom always complained that she didn't have enough money and it was always my fault.

"Of course I sent child support. I may not have wanted you, but I hold up to my responsibilities."

That one sentence was like a dagger to my heart. I was destroyed. I didn't say another word. I turned and marched back down the driveway of his super-expensive home in the elite neighborhood in south Tampa to my piece-of-crap car and drove away.

I never looked back. I also never dated another jock. If no one else would date a certain guy, I would, simply because I knew he was safe. I've never been conceited, but I knew that I was prettier than a lot of girls our age. The popular boys always asked me out, and I always turned them down. I didn't plan to live the same life as my mom, so I was going to stay away from any man that even resembled a younger version of my father.

Now, I have the ultimate popular boy—turned man—in front of me. Captain of the football team in high school, graduated second in his class he was so smart, and student body president. Now as an adult, it's worse. He was Army Special Forces and now works for one of the hottest security teams in the country. The man looks like he could be on the cover of *GQ Magazine* he's so good-looking. I know he's dated some pretty impressive women since he's been an adult—one of whom is an actress I admire. There's no way he'll want me long-term. I don't have anything that would keep him with me once he gets bored with the sex. If we remain only friends then I always get to keep him in my life, even if it's not in the way I really want.

The truth is I've had a quiet crush on Mike for almost as long as I've known him. But trying to have a relationship with a man as amazing as he is and having it fall apart, would not only kill me, it would end my friendship with his family. That's too much to lose. I have to find a way to avoid the subject of love until this mess is over, and he's gone back to his life. He'll remember then why us dating is a bad idea.

Once we're clean, we curl up in the spoon position and fall asleep, him holding me close, just the way I like it. That night, I sleep better than I have since the last time I lay in a bed with him.

THE NEXT DAY, Maggie gets bent out of shape again when Mike insists that I wait inside until the car arrives. My nerves are frayed, and two days of this ridiculous attitude from her is enough to get under my skin and fester. The car ride to the pier, where we're meeting the boat that's taking us to the Shadow Key filming location, is awkward. Maggie mutters under her breath the whole trip. Unable to take her shit anymore, I blurt, "I don't understand why you're so pissed, Maggie. Nothing about this is inconveniencing you, other than you get to ride in a car with a smoking hot guy. Your ire makes no sense. If this were your issue, I'd do anything and everything you needed to keep you safe, so shut up."

Both hers and Mike's eyes grow wide during my outburst. I'm not known for shooting off at the mouth. I learned after years of dealing with my mother that exercising patience is the only way to get through difficult situations. That theory has worked well since I started in this business. The temperamental actors, actresses, directors and photographers require this at times, and I'm good at it, but something about Maggie's attitude, while I'm under this kind of stress, is too much for me to deal with.

After my little outburst, the car is quiet. When Maggie

looks out the window to avoid me, Mike smiles and raises his eyebrows like I surprised him. I shrug and turn my focus to the road ahead. It shut her up so maybe I need to have those kinds of freak-outs more often.

———

THE HEAT and humidity were off the charts today, and those things coupled with the continuing tension between Maggie and me while filming has wiped me out. I hope Mike's okay with eating in the room again because I'm too tired to be vigilant while we go out somewhere.

After I've showered, and we've ordered our room service, I plop down on the couch and check my social media sites. My phone buzzes in my hand, showing that it's the executive producer of *Shadow Key*, Wallace Smythe. He's probably calling because Maggie complained. I hope so because I'll be glad to share what led to my outburst.

"Hey, it's Wallace. I'm sorry to bother you. I know you're tired after the long shoot today, but I wondered if we could meet in the lobby for a few minutes. I need to go over something with you."

Ugh. I'm so tired, and I don't feel like going down there to have a talk tonight, but he produces a lot of movies, and I want to make a good impression. Too many actresses I've worked with make everyone jump through hoops. I don't want to be one of those women, so I'm working hard to make a good name in this business. I glance at Mike, who's watching me closely, and say, "Sure. Give me a few minutes to get dressed." We finish the conversation quickly and I stand to get dressed.

"What's up, M?"

"That's Wallace, the producer. He wants to meet with me. Probably about the scenes for tomorrow or something. I'll be back in a few minutes."

"You're not going without me."

"It's just to the lobby. Seriously, just wait for our room service to show up and text me when it does. That will give me an excuse to cut it short."

"I'm here to protect you, not be your food boy," he says firmly with a hint of irritation.

"There's no threat. I've been eating in public for weeks since all this started. What's someone going to do to me in a crowded lobby? Besides, Wallace is a big guy, he can protect me for a few minutes." I kiss Mike quickly and walk out the door before he can argue more. The truth is that I'm starving, and I don't want to delay our dinner further by no one being in the room when it's delivered. I'm sure Mike will be pissed and give me a lecture when I get back, but at least I can eat while he does.

When I reach the lobby, I look around and see people everywhere, but none of them is Wallace. *Where the hell is he?* After a minute or so, my phone rings and his number pops up on the screen.

I answer and he says, "I'm standing right out front having a smoke. Can you meet me out here? It'll only take a minute."

Not wanting to hang out down here all night waiting for him to get his nicotine fix, even against my better judgment, I step out the door and look around. The orange glow of the cigarette at the end of the building gives him away, so I walk in his direction. When I'm close enough to see his face, he grins. At that moment, something connects with the back of my head, and I register the worst pain I've ever felt right before everything goes black.

———

MY HEAD IS POUNDING as I come to in a cramped dark space. Muffled music is thumping, shaking my whole body like the woofers at a dance club. I swallow the best I can, considering there's a wad of cloth shoved in my mouth, gagging the shit out of me. My mind is turtle slow as I attempt to process all these things together so I can understand what's going on.

Oh my God. Mike's probably crazy pissed and worried. I should've listened. Where am I and why does my head hurt so damn bad? Was it Wallace who put me here? It had to be. He's such a big guy that no one could have gotten past him unless he allowed it.

By the vibration under me, I'm guessing I'm in the trunk of a moving car. I hate confined spaces, and my chest heaves as a freak-out builds within. I'm in a trunk, Mike doesn't know where I am, and I'm probably going to die. What if Wallace wants to do something other than kill me? I'd rather die than be raped, and I'll go down fighting if that's what he has in mind. I never even got the creep vibe from Wallace, so I have no idea what's going on or if it really is him. I wish the music was lower, it's making my headache worse and I feel like I'm going to puke.

Why would Wallace hurt me like this? Is he the one who's been sending me all the crazy messages and the one who jacked off on my bed? All the notes were signed C and Wallace's initials are W.S. It doesn't make sense. Mike isn't going to know what happened to me. I should've listened to him. I brought him here to keep me safe, but when he tried, I ignored his warning because of all things I was hungry and now I'm probably going to die.

12

Mike

Damn it! I knew I should have gone with Summer. I ignored her instruction to stay in the room and was only about a minute or two behind her but she was already gone. As I was walking off the elevator, a young guy was running into the building, yelling that some lady got stuffed into a trunk, and I knew it was her. The bottom dropped out from under me when I heard it.

I sprinted outside, but they were long gone, so I went straight to the manager and asked him to pull the security footage. He tried to argue, but with some creative persuasion, he did what I asked and led me to his office. As the video played, I watched a small figure, distinctly feminine, but wearing jeans, a hoodie and sunglasses, come up behind Summer and hit her on the back of her head with a broom handle. She stumbled forward and dropped to the ground like she was out cold. Wallace and the woman shoved her into the back of an already running black Mercedes.

Insane rage exploded inside, consuming me. I wanted to punch my fist through the wall to relieve the tension. It took me a minute to regain my composure. I pulled out my phone and called my boss, Albert Ross, who co-owns Security Six with Amelia Desanto, to ask for help. Quickly, I explained my situation.

"I'm putting you on speaker. Amelia's here and I want her to hear everything. Relay the info slower while I run the plates you gave me," Albert says to me. "I'm calling Hudson in to help."

"He's on vacation; he was going to the Bahamas when he left us yesterday."

"He's decided to skip the vacation. He called this morning to tell me he's available if anything comes up. That guy has no idea how to relax."

Thank God for that because I'm going to need all the help I can get.

APPARENTLY, Wallace has a hunting cabin in southern Georgia and a beach house north of Hilton Head, so the Security Six team knew it was possible he was heading for one or the other. The unknown factors, like who he's working with and why he's doing this, left us unsure of other avenues he might take. The only reason we guessed the turnpike was because we figured he'd want the fastest route out of southern Florida.

Albert suggested Hudson and I stay in Key West in case the kidnappers hadn't left the Keys, but he dispatched team members to the rest stops on the south end of the turnpike just in case. Hudson is in the driver's seat of my jeep while I sit in the passenger seat waiting in the parking lot of the hotel staring at my phone, willing it to ring. After two and a half hours of twiddling our thumbs we get a call from Security Six headquarters in Tampa informing us that a car registered to

Wallace A. Smythe goes through the first toll plaza on the Florida Turnpike heading north.

The hotel manager and I called in the police, but they're slow to respond and have a hundred questions. Until they saw the hotel video, they kept saying they couldn't do anything. Not that I expect much out of them. I know their hands are tied with bureaucratic bullshit, whereas our security team has more resources and doesn't necessarily have to follow a bunch of rules to take care of business. When the police left the hotel, I didn't have a good feeling that they would find Summer before we did, but I was willing to ask anyone and everyone who would listen to try.

Things got worse for me right after the police understood that my accusations were real and put out an alert to all Florida counties through their sheriff's office. My parents got the notifications and were calling to put me on the case. Getting them off the phone so I could work on things was tough. Like I mentioned before, Summer grew up in our house, she's one of us, and my parents freaked out.

When I finally located contact information for Phil Harmon and was able to explain the situation, he lost his mind. I heard he was temperamental, but this was something else entirely. At first, he was freaking out because it would delay the shooting schedule and then it was because it would draw bad press. When I finally had enough of his selfish bullshit and reminded him that one of the actresses might actually die he seemed to get it and broke down in tears over the phone. It took a few minutes to calm him down.

It was during the first part of his freak-out that he revealed Maggie had left the set early, saying she thought she had food poisoning. That got my brain moving, and I realized where I'd seen the person in the surveillance video with Wallace. She had on a wig, hat and sunglasses, but her gait was unmistakable. That bitch helped, and she better hope I'm not the one to find her because, for the first time in my life, I know I'll not only hit a woman but I'll hit first and ask questions later. I text Albert to let him know Maggie is the accomplice.

Now that Hudson and I know Wallace and Maggie are indeed heading north on the turnpike, we take off in that direction. Sitting in Key West waiting for someone else to find her isn't an option.

An hour and a half later, we're almost out of the Keys when we get a phone call from Albert.

"We've got Summer, but Wallace and Maggie got away." I breathe a sigh of relief but immediately worry about Summer's well-being.

"How is she? Is she okay?"

"She has a head injury and she's freaked out, but she's alive and alert. Wallace didn't want her pissing in the car, so they pulled her from the trunk, thinking they could take her to the bathroom and put her right back inside the car. He never pegged Summer for a fighter."

Like a giant pussy I'm ready to cry, but instead laugh out loud. The month before Summer and Valerie entered high school, my brother Thomas and I taught them how to fight back if they were ever attacked. I knew I would be around for a lot of stuff with them, but not necessarily if they ended up on a date gone bad or even at a party I wasn't attending. We drilled them for weeks and it's finally paid off nearly 30 years later.

"Amelia was at that particular rest stop when Summer finally got a chance to fight back. Amelia got her out of there but couldn't grab Wallace and Maggie at the same time. At least we have Summer, but we're now on the hunt for Wallace and Maggie. How far away are you?"

"We're a little south of Miami now. Can you take Summer back to Tampa? I'll have the hotel manager box up our stuff in Key West and overnight it to our headquarters. I want her where I can keep her safe. The filming will already be on hold until she recovers and Maggie is replaced."

"Yeah, we thought having her at your place was the was the best idea too. You ready to talk to her?"

"Yes." I switch from Bluetooth speaker to handset and listen as her quiet, shaken voice comes on the line.

"Sweetheart, you okay?"

"I don't know. I'm so sorry. I should've listened to you. I should've let you come with me and not worried about room service." She starts crying in earnest now.

"Don't cry. I'm not mad at you. I was scared shitless, but never mad at you. I am going to kill those fuckers myself for putting you through this, though. Did they ever say why they were doing this?"

"They owe some guy named C a favor. Wallace is afraid of him and Maggie's just plain crazy. She just kept prattling about 'making it big' and I didn't understand. I was in the trunk until they stopped at the rest stop. There's something extra crazy to all of this that I'm missing, but whatever it is, I want to get away from it. When are you coming for me? I need you." Her voice breaks on the last word, and it takes everything in me to sound strong when I reply.

"I know, sweetheart. Go with Amelia to Tampa, and I'll meet you there as soon as I can. Probably about four hours. Follow any instructions she gives you, and they'll take care of you."

"Okay," she says quietly.

"I love you, M. It's going to be okay. I'll make sure of it." I disconnect and look at Hudson. "You need to pick up the pace, man. Listening to her cry . . ."

He doesn't respond, he just floors it and the angry growl of my jeep engine mirrors my own thoughts.

IN THREE AND A HALF HOURS, Hudson and I pull up to Security Six headquarters. Amelia's SUV is parked out front but Albert's is gone. Randy Feldman—one of the guys on the security team—is parked next to Amelia. We climb out of the jeep and use my keys to enter the old warehouse building.

When I stalk through the door, my eyes are wild as they seek out Summer. As soon as she spots me, she's out of her seat and in my arms. "Oh God, Mike, I'm so scared."

I hold her tighter, hoping to convey that I won't let her go again. "I know, M, but I've got you. None of this will happen again. You've got my word. We have a lot to talk about, but we'll do it in the morning. Tonight, we need some sleep, so let's head to my place. At least that way I know we have proper security for the night."

I turn to see who's in the room with us and find Randy and Hudson talking quietly off to the side across from us. When Randy and I make eye contact, he says, "Hey. I'll give Hudson a ride to his apartment. You can pick him up on your way here in the morning."

I'd forgotten he left his car in Key West. They walk over to where we're standing.

"Sounds good. Thanks for everything, guys. I'll rent you a car to get you back to yours, Hudson."

"Nah, man, my cousin is going to drive it up tomorrow and hang here at the beach for a few days until I go back."

I nod, appreciating the fact that I don't have to worry about that. "Randy, I thought you were off this week. Why are you here and where are Amelia and Albert?"

"I know what it's like to have someone you care about be in trouble. I came in to help, and I'll be here all week if I need to be. I'll check in with you tomorrow. Amelia and Albert are headed to Wallace's cabin in Georgia. They're pretty certain the guy is dumb enough to go there. If they don't find him there, they're headed to Hilton Head. Albert will call you first thing in the morning. Go get some rest."

Shaking hands with both men, I pause longer with Hudson. "Thanks, man. I can't say it enough."

"Don't mention it. We'll see you in the morning. Take care of her tonight."

I nod and lead Summer to the jeep with my hand at the small of her back. The way her shoulders are slumped over, I can tell she's tired. I can't wait to get her home and in bed, just so I can hold her while she sleeps.

When we get to my house, I let Scooter out quickly before I snag a T-shirt from my drawer and lead Summer to the shower. I had it redone when I bought the place. The entire thing, including the ceiling, is covered in porcelain tiles. The three showerheads will make it easier for us to shower together without one of us being out of the water. I turn them on and set the temperature. As she removes her clothes, I notice several scratches and a ton of bruises, and the rage builds again. I haven't seen the head injury yet, but I know it's there. Once the temperature is right, I drop my clothes in a heap on the floor and lead her into the shower. I pour shower gel into my hands and rub them together before I begin the gentle washing of Summer's skin from neck to toes. She moans softly, not in a sexual way, but in more of a soul-gaining-comfort kind of way. When I finish with her body, I wash her hair, being careful to avoid her head injury.

Once she's rinsed, I scrub myself quickly as she relaxes under the spray. When we're done, I step out first and wrap a towel around my waist. Scooter, who followed me into the bathroom, is still lying inside the doorway waiting for us. He knows when Summer's around she spoils him and it's obvious he doesn't plan to miss out on that.

Carefully, I wrap a towel around her shoulders as she exits. Summer remains quiet the whole time we're drying off, almost shell-shocked. I shuffle the T-shirt over her head and lead her to my bed. While she's climbing under the covers, I tug on some boxer briefs and turn out the lights. I'm ready to join her when she asks, "Can you lift Scooter up here to lie with me?" It's been a crazy day for me, and I've been so focused on Summer that I forgot to do that already.

"Yeah, I'll grab him." I grab the chunky hound and I lower him to her side of the bed. He makes two circles before plopping down so she can spoon him. I slide in behind Summer, wrap an arm around her waist to secure her to me, and kiss her hair. It's not long before I can feel her body shake as she cries, so I hold her tight and let her get it out. After a little bit, she finally settles down to just the sniffles and rolls over to face me.

"I was so afraid I'd never get to tell you that I love you. I should have said it when you told me. I knew it then, but I was scared."

"You've got nothing to be afraid of. I've loved you for a long time, and I've got no intention of stopping any time soon."

"You know about my dad, right?"

"Yeah, sweetheart, I know about that piece of shit and I'm nothing like him."

"I know, but I'm still afraid. You could have anyone. I'm nothing special."

"Don't ever say that shit again. You're beautiful, you're smart, you're talented and you're my best friend. You have been for years. You're already part of my family in a way no one else could be. I wouldn't pursue you if it was a fling. There is no way I would risk our friendship if this wasn't real for me. I've got dreams of forever, sweetheart. You know the kind of family I come from. You should have no doubt."

"I love you, Mike. I have for a long time, too."

I kiss her soft and slow, our tongues dancing perfectly

together. When I end the kiss on a soft peck, I tell her, "Get some rest, sweetheart. We'll have a long day tomorrow."

"You don't want to . . ."

"You need rest and healing. We have the rest of our lives to make love. Part of loving you is doing what's best for you no matter what I want. I want to take care of you. Let me, please."

"Okay," she whispers as she burrows into my chest. "We need to call your sister Valerie and your parents tomorrow. My mom won't give a crap, but yours will, and since the police were involved, I'm certain it'll be all over the gossip sites at least."

"I already talked to my dad. As soon as the alert went out for you, he was on the phone telling me to find you. He didn't realize it was my fault it had happened. They know you're okay and will be checking in tomorrow. We can call Val in the morning, if they haven't already."

"You think it's your fault?"

"Of course it's my fault. My job is high-level security. I'm supposed to be an expert at keeping someone safe, and I let you walk to the lobby unaccompanied to meet with someone I haven't done a background check on. That's amateur hour."

"But I didn't want you to go. I told you no."

"If I was doing my job instead of trying to make you happy, that never would've happened."

"But—"

"No buts. Now get some sleep. I have a feeling we'll need it until this is taken care of."

We settle in and I sleep lightly, on edge, listening to every little sound throughout the night. Scooter's snoring breaks up the quiet some, but not enough to put me at ease. I'll do everything in my power to keep Summer safe and if that means lack of sleep, so be it. She, on the other hand, sleeps like the dead and I'm so thankful she's comfortable enough to sleep well.

THE NEXT DAY, Summer and I talk to a Key West detective who tells us that the case has been turned over to the FBI. We have to enlist Roman Porter, the computer expert from work, to check those files the covert way. She used to do the same job for the Tampa police department but is now part of our team. She's a genius hacker and can break into any system, anywhere, and get us the info we need.

Our biggest problem is that we have no idea who this C person is, so we don't know who we're looking for. My gut tells me that it's someone Summer knows, has probably worked with and that makes me more nervous. She's so sweet and unassuming that she'd never suspect anyone and trusts everyone, unless she's slapped in the face with their betrayal.

Summer is in Amelia's office working on her social media presence and catching up on her emails while Randy, Roman and I discuss who C could be in the conference room.

"The problem is Summer's popularity has exploded in the last six months. Everyone wants her. The indie authors, the magazines, and now even Hollywood is jumping on board. She's got it coming from all sides, and she won't say no to any of them," I tell the group.

Roman looks thoughtful for a moment before finally saying, "I'd start with the director, Phil Harmon. Maybe he's become obsessed with her. The way he discovered her is not the normal Hollywood success story."

"Already did a basic check," I say. My gut says it's not him. When I called him in the beginning he was too freaked out. I think we're looking for someone on the inside of the industry, but not quite that close to her. I'm not sure how things work exactly, but maybe office personnel for the film company, or a driver, or someone from catering that comes near Summer, but has never been close enough to be on her radar. You can check

Harmon out to be safe, but I really don't think it's him. Do you understand what I'm saying?"

Randy squints for a second as he thinks. "Yeah, I get what you're saying, but to isolate some possibilities, we're going to have to throw out a wide net. I was hoping it would be a little more obvious."

"Nothing is ever that easy." I turn to Roman. "I'd like you to start looking into any company associated with *Shadow Key*. We're looking for a name that starts with a C. Could be first, middle, or last. I'm going to be digging into all the photographers and writers she's worked with. Randy, see if you can figure out who Maggie has been linked to for friendships and relationships in Hollywood. She's tied to this somehow, and we may be able to find it through her. For the time being, Summer goes nowhere alone. If it's not necessary, she doesn't go out at all. The last two idiots that grabbed her were amateurs, but I doubt the next person will be stupid enough to make the same mistakes."

Everyone nods in agreement, so I stand and work my way through the building to Amelia's office. When I approach, I can see that Summer's brow is pinched in concentration and concern. I lean over and kiss her hair and back off just a little bit, holding steady as I wait for her to tilt her head and face me. As soon as she does, I kiss her softly and hold for a second longer than normal, just savoring the taste of her. God, I've been waiting for a ridiculous amount of time to be able to walk into a room and kiss her without thinking twice. My parents are going to be thrilled when they find out we're together. I think they've probably wanted this as long as I have. They love her and consider her family already.

"What's wrong?" I ask her.

"I don't like the negative attention this is getting me. I don't want to be known as a drama magnet. I want to be known for the right things. This career is something I've wanted for so long and never thought would be possible. I'd hate it if something I can't even control causes me to lose it all." The tension in her raised shoulders is obvious, so I step behind her and knead the muscles.

"M, we're going to take care of this. Give us a little time. Phil Harmon found *you*, remember that. He won't set you aside that easy. Believe in yourself like I believe in you." I pause for a moment and let that sink in before I continue with a different subject. "Listen, my parents are going to want to see you. Are you okay with stopping by their house on the way back to my place?"

"Is Security Six going to be okay with that?"

"I'm in charge of your personal safety for the night so I say it's okay. I doubt anyone could anticipate us going there."

"Yes, I could use a dose of good reality. I can call this reality, but it's not a good one."

I kiss her shoulder and step back. "We've got a plan, but it's going to take us awhile. Are you good in here?"

She nods and gives me a small smile. "Thanks for taking care of me."

"Anything for you." I say before I get to work trying to figure this out.

Roman, Randy, and I spend the afternoon vetting all personnel we can find with any affiliation to the film Summer's been in and all photographers she's been associated with. By the time we're done, we only have a handful of people left and a handful of possibilities that we need to dig into further. Roman is planning to get a little sleep and then jump back on it.

———

JUST LIKE I always do at my parents' house, I knock twice and open the door, ready to walk right in. Before we can get inside, my mom has Summer wrapped in a tight embrace.

"Mom, you can hug her inside. I don't want Summer out here in the open."

"Yes, you're right. Sorry. Come on in," my mom says as she ushers us in.

Once we're in the door, Mom grabs Summer's arm to stop her. Gently, Mom places her hands on Summer's shoulders and looks down at her. Mom is a good four inches taller than Summer. "When we turned on the news and heard you'd been taken, I . . . well, let's just say it wasn't a good night. I'm so glad you're home, and I'm glad to finally see one of my boys wise up." Mom glances at me and then pulls us both in for a hug and holds tight. "I love you both." The slight shake to her voice tells me she's barely holding it together. She kisses both of our heads in a very motherly fashion. "As soon as your dad told me you were coming, I made your favorite, Summer, spaghetti and homemade garlic bread."

"Have I told you lately how awesome you are?" Summer asks her.

My mom beams, pleased she made Summer happy. My dad finally approaches and grips her by the shoulders, too, and looks her over, head to toe. Not like a man perusing the body of a woman, but like a man checking his daughter for visible signs she's hurt. There are only a couple that can be seen with her clothes on, thank goodness. He lets go of her shoulders and tips her chin up with his fingers so he can look into her eyes. "We love you, kiddo. Don't know what we'd do without you."

My dad never gets choked up, but he certainly is right now. To end his unusual show of emotion, he hugs her as gently as a six-feet-four beast of a man can. I get my size and shape from him. Even in his late 60s, he's still strong and fit, and I hope that carries through in the genes too. I follow Mom into the kitchen while Dad finishes talking to Summer.

"How long has this been going on?" Mom whispers and gestures between Summer and me.

"It's new, Mom. We tried when we came back from helping Val last spring, but her schedule was crazy, and I had several big cases come up, so we couldn't make it work."

"You're 45 years old, Michael James. If you take too long getting your stuff figured out, I'll never get any more grand-kids. I don't see Thea enough as it is. Besides, I want Summer-and-Michael grandbabies."

"Mom, you're moving a little fast."

She turns to me and puts her hand on her hip, her eyes narrowing dangerously. "Michael, you've had over 35 years to get to know her. I'd say that you have no clue what fast is."

"Thirty-five years for what?" Summer asks as she strolls into the kitchen with my dad on her heels.

"To finally get together with you," my mother snaps sounding exasperated.

Summer stops dead in her tracks, and at first, I think she's going to freak out in a bad way, and then she says, "I had to let him get the entire high school cheerleading squad out of his system before I'd accept a date." My mouth drops open. *Did she really say that to my parents?*

Both of my parents double over with laughter, and I stand looking at all of them like they're crazy. "I didn't date the cheerleading squad." Well not all of them.

My mom sets the spoon on the stove and turns to me with her eyebrows raised. "Let's review." She looks at the ceiling as if she's working hard to remember before she focuses on me again. "Margo, Jessica B., Jessica M., Kara, Cindy, Lindy, Marie, Marnie, Brooke and the one with the overly teased bangs and heavy eye shadow, whose name I can't recall. The only one left was . . ." She points at Summer who's smiling and fighting laughter like this is hysterical.

"That's not even everyone he dated, that's only the cheer squad," Summer reminds my parents.

"You were a little busy, son," Dad reminds me.

Slightly embarrassed, but remembering that my parents forgot about a huge part of the equation, I point out, "Look at Summer's dates through high school, and we'll all remember why I never bothered to ask. I didn't stand a chance. She liked scrawny and brainy, or scrawny and thespian. A guy like me couldn't compete with either."

The color leaves her face, and her eyes shift to the floor. The whole room goes quiet. I've hit a nerve and we all know it. I should have kept my mouth shut. We all know about her father, but we never discuss it in front of her and this is why.

"You know I was afraid I'd end up with someone like my dad. I avoided the guys who had it all."

The spaghetti sauce pops behind Mom on the stove, but it's quiet otherwise. No one says anything for long awkward seconds. Finally, I step up close to her, ignoring the fact that my parents are standing here for all of this. I was the idiot who made it weird while the rest of them were just joking.

"M, look at me." When she lifts her gaze to meet mine, her eyes are swimming in unshed tears. "Your dad is a fuckwad. No man worth his salt would desert his baby girl and her mother, especially when that baby girl was you. I love you, and I'm not going anywhere and not out of a sense of obligation. I'm here because I've loved you for years. As long as you'll have me, I'll be right by your side. I'm talking forever. Career, kids and old folks' homes. Every bit of it. Don't you see? I've been waiting for you for years. Not just someone, or someone like you. I've been waiting for *you*."

"Mike," she breathes as the tears trickle down her face. I take her cheeks in my hands and kiss her until I hear Mom squeak next to me, and I remember that we're in my parents' kitchen. I back off and glance at Mom who's also crying.

"Josh, I'm finally getting my wish," Mom says to Dad as he wraps an arm around her.

I can't help but comment too. "Me too, Mom, me too." I kiss Summer's forehead and step away to help set the table.

Dinner is wonderful as usual, and after the initial excitement ends, we fade into our normal family pattern, laughing and talking about anything and everything. I wish Thomas, Valerie and Thea were here. That's when it would feel perfect.

13

Summer

I jump off of Mike's chest like I'm being burned, scaring Scooter and causing him to bark, when Mike's phone rings at 3:30 in the morning. *Who sets their ringtone to the actual ringing sound?*

"Wade," he says groggily as he answers it. There's a long silence as he listens.

"So where is she?" A sound similar to a growl comes from him. I rest on my elbow, looking down at him, trying to decipher facial expressions in the dark room. It's fruitless but it's giving me something to do.

"Did he say where he thinks she is? Why isn't he talking?" More silence. "The police won't be able to do shit. He'll lawyer up and we won't get information in enough time to help us. Fuck! Did you get any info from him?"

My heart is hammering in my chest because I know they're talking about Wallace and Maggie.

"It was him?" There is a pause before he mutters, "Sick fucker. Fine. See you in a few hours. Thanks for finding him."

Him? Not them?

When he hangs up, he reaches over toward the bedside

table and pauses to inform me, "I'm turning on the light." I close my eyes and wait a second, then I blink rapidly, allowing my eyes to adjust.

"What's going on?" I ask, unable to hide the fear.

"They have Wallace. Amelia and Albert caught him trying to get into his cabin in southern Georgia. Apparently, the guy is a dumbass, definitely not a criminal mastermind. He was only doing what Maggie told him to do. He's been wanting to fuck Maggie for a while, and she offered him what he wanted if he helped get you to C. The police have Wallace in custody but Albert says he's too scared to talk. Whoever this C character is, he has him terrified."

"Why did you call him a sick fucker?"

"He was the one who jacked off on your bed. Maggie told him it would really freak you out."

"Well, she was right even as disgusting as that was. What does all this mean for me?" Hoping he has good news but knowing that he won't.

"It means we stay vigilant. You remain under security until we catch Maggie and C. We will, it may just take longer than we expected."

"I knew something was up with Maggie, but I never dreamed she would be behind any of this. I just thought she was a temperamental pain in the butt. Why does it have to be so complicated? I'm sorry. I've ruined your time off and you're stuck with me."

"You haven't ruined anything. Did you not listen to what I said yesterday? I've been waiting for years for you. I'll give up every vacation from now until I die if it means I have you."

"I love you, Mike," I whisper, the emotion overpowering my voice.

"I love you too, sweetheart."

Scooter must sense what's coming because he moves to the foot of the bed as far from us as he can get and lies down.

Leaning over, I kiss Mike, pouring every ounce of heart and soul into the kiss as I explore his mouth with my tongue. With a quick adjustment of my hips, I pull my mouth away as I straddle him, centering myself over his cock, slipping him inside me. He's watching me with the sexiest hooded eyes as I sink all the way down on him. My head falls back and I moan as he fills me almost to the point of discomfort. He tugs the T-shirt over my head and tosses it to the floor, then runs his hands from my bare hips over my rib cage to thumb and pinch my nipples. I can't help but arch into his expert touch. I rise and fall on him with ease as my pussy gets wetter and wetter with his work at my breasts. Mike is a genius with his fingers.

The harder I rise and fall on him, the more his hips lift to meet mine. We have a punishing rhythm and we work in perfect synchronicity. I'm getting close, so I lean forward and brace myself on his chest as my core flutters and grips him, and I come in a chorus of curse words and praises all mixed in together. Then I brace myself as he continues pounding up into me until he finally flexes one last time and holds, filling me full.

When he flips me, managing to somehow stay inside me, he looks into my eyes and says, "I want you to marry me, M."

"Mike . . ." I say, suddenly terrified. "We're so new."

"I'm not asking right now. Not like this. But we're light years from new and you know it. We've been close for years. Best friends most of that time. The chemistry is there. The sex is beyond amazing. I've loved you for so long, and I know you love me too. There's no reason we shouldn't. People search their whole lives to find a fraction of what we have and never get it. Prepare yourself because when the time is right. I will be asking. You're it for me."

"What about my career? It's just now getting started."

"I want that for you as bad as you want it. Having a baby

might be something we have to work around your schedule since we are both older, but you do want kids, right?"

I nod slowly.

"Then a career shouldn't stop us from having each other."

He kisses me soft and quick and moves off of me. I stare after his retreating outline and wonder how I got lucky enough that my sexy, amazing best friend wants to marry me. But can I trust this? Nothing this good ever happens to me. There's no way that after having nothing for years—a crap job, no future, no kids of my own, no husband or even a boyfriend—I can be getting everything I want almost all at once.

He comes back with a damp washrag in his hand and says, "Spread your legs, sweetheart."

I spread my legs and watch as his eyes go from sleepy and sated to hot in a second. I can't help but grin. I've never seen anything like that before.

"It's got to be a caveman thing," he remarks.

"What?"

"The fact that I started to get hard again when I saw my cum leaking out of you. It felt like I slapped an ownership badge on you, and it turned me the fuck on."

I laugh out loud as he leans in and gently cleans me up.

"You have the goofiest laugh. You know that, right?" he asks, chuckling.

I do my best to look offended but can't pull it off. I know I have the kind of laugh that makes other people laugh. I tried to fix it growing up, but it never worked. I always reverted back to this so now I just accept it. "Yeah, I know. Hell, your family has teased me about it for years." I do my best to look pissed, and he throws the rag toward the bathroom and leaps onto the bed, poking me in the ribs with his middle finger right away. I squeal and laugh louder. Scooter joins the noise with his deep bark, and just like that, I forget to be scared that crazy people are out to get me. When my laughter subsides, he kisses me long and deep and rolls me to my side so he can spoon me. It's my favorite way to sleep with him. Safe, up close and still able to cuddle Scooter, who waddled back to curl up next to me.

———

THE NEXT DAY, Mike and I meet with Albert and Amelia at his office headquarters, and I can't help but be impressed with those two. Both are knowledgeable and focused without losing personality, and I enjoy watching them work, but after a while, I realize I need to find something productive to do. Amelia puts me in her office again to check email and peruse my social media sites. The second message I open is from Simone.

Hey. I hope you're okay. I saw all the stuff on the news and tried to text you but didn't get a response. I understand if you need to cancel, but that signing I had you scheduled for is in Tampa this weekend. Let me know if you're in or not. I had a few people coming to meet you specifically. If you can't make it, I may see if we can meet up, so I can have you sign books for those people.

Mike walks in and kisses my head. "What's up? Roman says you have some messages on social media, but they all look benign. She also says you have an obligation coming up."

"I'm just reading that now. In the middle of all of this, I forgot. I was scheduled to have a break and planned to be at Simone's book signing."

"I'm going to advise against it."

"I have to be there, Mike. If it weren't for her putting me on her cover, I wouldn't have every opportunity I have now. I have to repay that. It'll affect her sales if I don't show. You can go with me and stay by my side through the whole thing if you don't have other plans. I know you were supposed to be on vacation."

With a raised eyebrow, he studies me and then replies. "My

vacation would have consisted of sitting on a beach doing nothing, having dinner with my parents a time or two, and if nothing came up with work, I was going to surprise Val in Colorado. That's it. If it's that important to you to be at the signing, I'll be your bodyguard."

"It's that important."

"Done, but I need to check with Hudson to see if he can go too, and I'll need the schedule of events so I'm prepared. The fewer surprises, the better."

"Did I tell you I love you yet today?" I ask as I smile up at him.

"Yes, after I made love to you for the second time." His smile is smug before he kisses me hard, then turns and struts out of the room like a man who knows he owns my body. If I weren't a grown-ass woman, I'd swoon.

OVER THE NEXT SEVERAL DAYS, there's no sign of Maggie, and we still aren't any closer to figuring out who C is. The morning of the signing we meet up with Hudson—who insisted on coming—to grab some gear. Apparently, each man is going to have an earpiece communication device, and they have some other things going on that I don't know about but that Mike says will be subtle and unobtrusive. Whatever they want to do is fine with me as long as I can help my friend.

Mike, Hudson and I check in at 11 a.m. in the Marriot hotel lobby where the book signing is being held. Once we're finished Mike and I walk hand in hand while Hudson stays a few feet behind us until we reach the ballroom. Inside the room is bustling with activity because the 50 authors, models and vendors are setting up their tables with books and swag for the hundreds of readers we're expecting today. I locate Simone and wave as we approach. Her eyes practically bulge out of her head when she gets a look at Mike.

"Simone, meet Mike my boyfriend slash bodyguard."

Her grin grows as she realizes what I've said. Simone and I have been friends for five years, and I've never had a boyfriend during that time. I just couldn't date men I wasn't attracted to and the kind of guys I was willing to date, I really wasn't attracted to physically. For years, I was willing to fake it so I wasn't alone, but at some point, I couldn't do it anymore. It's not that I'm a huge prize or anything. I'm short with big natural boobs, but I have virtually no butt and short legs. They aren't fat, they're toned, but I'm not model material. How I ended up being one, I'll never understand. If you ask me, my best feature is my hair. I have thick blonde hair that's always shiny with a little bit of wave but not so much that it's unruly. Everything else is just average. I got lucky with the photos and movies in that people were searching for my exact look. As far as the acting, I've taken a million classes and do feel like I have skill in that department, but when it comes to looks, I'm only average.

"Well, hello, Mike the bodyguarding boyfriend. I'm Simone Sayer. Nice to meet you. Got any brothers?"

Mike laughs and replies, "Actually I do. Maybe you should meet him."

I turn to Mike with a huge grin. Why didn't I think of that before? "Oh my gosh! Yes! She's perfect for Thomas!"

"Well then, make it happen, girly," says Simone. Can't believe you've been holding out on me."

"I never thought about it until now. He's 40 though, which is a little older than you usually like them," I remind her.

"I like them all ages. I don't discriminate. But I prefer them hot, athletic and smart. That's a hard combo to find after age 30, it seems. They're either good-looking and dumb or smart and physically fragile. To find all three would be the trifecta. There's no way there are two of you in the same family."

Mike grins at her. "Actually, there are three of us, but the middle one is a girl. Summer's other best friend since we were kids. Thomas just retired from the army and hasn't lost the physique."

"Any time you're ready to make introductions, I am. Thank you so much for coming today. I know with everything going on it wasn't easy."

"It's cool. As long as I have my trusty bodyguard with me everything will be okay."

Simone glances over her shoulder and back at Mike. "Make yourself comfortable. You can sit in one of the chairs or we can work something out. Just let me know where you need to be. Mike looks the table over. A six-foot-tall banner with her name and tag line on it is standing about a foot behind the table. There are two folding chairs behind the table and not much room otherwise.

"Where will you be, M?"

"I'll probably stand in front of the table and slightly to the side. People like to come over and talk and take pictures while getting their books signed so it's easier."

He nods and stands there quietly for a moment contemplating all of this. "Okay, I'll sit behind the table to stay out of the way."

"Okay, thank you." I move in close and rise on my toes to place a quick kiss to his lips.

At noon, when the doors open, I notice Mike's shoulders tense a little when he sees the large number of people strolling in, but he stays behind the table, seated and alert. Hudson is back a little in a corner with a full view of our row and partial view of other rows, watching from a different angle. I feel safe with these men protecting me, so I relax and enjoy.

After two hours, there's finally a lull in traffic down our

aisle, so I excuse myself to the bathroom with Mike as my escort. There are two women standing near the door talking about a book one of them is holding, but no one else is nearby. Mike stops next to the women and puts on his most charming smile. Their eyes light up instantly. It's hilarious how quickly this works.

"Hi, ladies. I was wondering if I could get you to do us a favor?"

"What is it?" the lady who is obviously most interested asks.

"Can you peek in the ladies' room and tell me if anyone is in there? I can't send her in there without checking first, and I don't want to be ungentlemanly by barging in."

The two ladies turn their attention to me for a moment, and the brunette's eyes widen in recognition. "You're that movie star who was on the news the other night. You got kidnapped, right? Are you okay?"

Irritation pricks under my skin. This is the kind of attention I didn't want, but I don't want to come across like a bitch so I push the feeling aside. "Yes, I'm okay, thanks to this guy." I lean in closer so Mike's forced to put his arm around me. Don't ask me why I suddenly want these women to know he's taken, but I do. "Since the police haven't caught the kidnappers, though, he's making sure I'm safe."

They both nod like they understand. "Okay, I'll go check," the blonde one says and hustles away.

We all stand there quietly waiting the 30 seconds it takes for her to come back.

"It's all clear, she can go in," she yells across the open space as she comes back through the door.

"I'm going in with you," he says.

"You can't listen to me pee," I say, horrified at the thought. What if a fart sneaks out or something?

"That's nonnegotiable. Besides, I've heard you pee a hundred times before. You camped with our family for years."

I huff because I don't want to deal with an argument, but I'm not happy.

"We weren't dating any of those times." My eyes narrow as he grins at me.

"Doesn't matter, M. I've still heard it. It's not going to kill either one of us for me to hear it, so get in there and get this over with."

I grumble all the way to the stall. Once I've done my business, washed my hands and returned to my table, the crowd picks up. Only two hours left before this is over. Mike excuses himself to the bathroom when we return to the table and instructs me not to move because Hudson is watching.

When I turn back around after taking a swig of my water, a young girl, probably only 15 or 16 years old, stands in front of me and hands me a note. "Don't tell anyone," she says and scampers off.

I open the note and read.

Come to the back door near the pool. Alone. I've got your mother, and I have no problem taking her out. You've got five minutes.

My heart rate speeds up and panic sets in. I may not like my mom very much, but I don't want anything to happen to her. If I wait for Mike, it may be longer than five minutes. If I try to signal Hudson, whoever has her may find out and do something to her. I don't know what to do, and the panic is clouding my thought process. I turn to Simone and say, "Give this to Mike as soon as he gets back. I have to go." Then I run through the hall and out a side door toward the pool area, praying the whole time that Mike or Hudson gets to us before anything happens again. I don't want to end up in another trunk. I doubt it'll end as well as it did last time.

As I reach the glass doors and push through, I'm sweating and on high alert. I scan the pool deck where kids are splashing in the water and adults are sunning themselves. A woman wearing a huge straw hat and a black cover-up stands from the closest chair and walks toward me. The closer she gets, the easier she is to recognize. Maggie. Shit.

"Where's my mom?" I demand to know.

"Follow me and you'll see her in a minute. Make a scene and you won't see her again . . . ever," she says with a spooky calm voice that I hadn't expected.

"Maggie, why are you doing this? I thought we were friends."

"I don't make friends with people trying to take my job," she growls.

"I don't want your job. Our roles were already cast."

"Shut up and follow me or your mom is a memory."

A chill runs down my spine at her words, delivered so callously. Panic and anger are warring emotions within me. When we reach the parking lot, she leads me to a black SUV with dark windows and opens the back door. "Get in."

I pause, knowing if I get in, it's likely I'll never get out.

"Not until you show me my mom."

"Just get in the car, bitch," she barks as she pushes me. I stumble and fall forward, landing with my forearms on the seat of the SUV. When I look up, my mom is already inside, leaning against the window, strapped in with a seat belt and passed out like she's had too much to drink. She doesn't look like she was forced into the vehicle. It looks like she was out drinking with a friend and is now being driven home.

Maggie's swimsuit cover-up brushes the back of my thigh, and I'm brought back to why I'm here. I kick back hard like a donkey, knocking her off-balance. While she's falling back, I turn and barrel into her. Both of us go skidding across the pavement, ripping skin off of my arm and knee. She screams out as her head cracks against the asphalt, and I scramble off her, ready to run away when Hudson appears above Maggie with his gun aimed right at her face. Behind him are Mike and several people from the signing, including Simone and the lady whose table was next to ours. Relief washes over me like a wave.

Hudson places a boot in the middle of Maggie's chest to hold her where she is. "Don't think about moving, bitch," he rumbles.

Mike turns to me and yells, "Why did you follow her? You knew not to move!"

I understand that he's upset, but I don't deal well with this kind of reaction. "She said she had my mom and was going to kill her!"

"Your mom would've left you if the situation was reversed!"

"It doesn't matter! She's! My! Mom!" I scream back while the adrenaline continues to pulse through me. How can he yell at me during a time like this? My chest is heaving I'm so angry at this whole situation.

Hudson pulls handcuffs out of his pocket after flipping Maggie to her belly and clicks them on her wrists. Then he lifts her to her feet. At that point, Mike gets in her face, close enough that he could kiss her. "Who the fuck is C?"

She purses her lips tight, not ready to talk.

"Maybe you haven't figured it out yet, but you're up shit creek. There isn't a cop here yet, and I don't quite follow the rules of the law when it comes to taking care of her." He points at me angrily. Maggie stays quiet and Mike says to Hudson, "Toss her into the rear of my truck and let's take her to interrogation." Her eyes widen when she looks over at Mike's covered truck bed, and she shakes her head. "I can't tell you. He's dangerous. If I don't come back with Summer, my career is over."

"Lady, I don't give two turds about your career. You've abducted my girl once and tried a second time. I'm done being nice. Tell me what I need to know, or you're about to disappear." The couple of people that followed Mike are standing back a little, their mouths agape. I can't tell if they're taking mental notes for their next stories, or so they can give an accurate police report.

Maggie remains tight-lipped, so Hudson pulls her roughly to the truck. As he's gripping her waist and lifting her into the truck, she must realize no one plans to stop him so she screams, "Fine! I'll tell you, but you're ruining my career."

"I don't give a damn about your career. Start talking," Hudson tells her.

"Jean-Christophe Cadieux." She practically yells the words at him.

Oh my God! My stomach rolls over.

Mike's right eyebrow raises. "The French director?" He looks at me like he's trying to figure out what Cadieux has to do with me. I don't think I ever told Mike anything about that.

I forgot all about Cadieux, but it makes sense now. Swallowing back the rising bile, I explain, "He wanted me for a movie that borders on porn, and I declined. I had no interest. We met at a red-carpet event, and he kind of gave me the creeps, so when he sent the script over for me to look at, I was already leaning toward saying no. I did eventually read it, but that made it clearer. There was no way I was doing that movie. Cadieux wouldn't allow for a body double during the sex scenes, and they were explicit." I turn to Maggie. "Did he think he could force me to do the movie?"

"Oh yes, he still plans to make sure you do the movie, but he also wants you to star in his personal home movie," Maggie spits, obviously jealous—though I have no idea why. That guy is crazy and creepy.

"Neither of those things are ever going to happen."

"Oh please, there's no way an old-ass bitch like you got the role you're in now without sucking a dick or two. Why wouldn't you just fuck him?" Rage burns through me. I'm so tired of people assuming I slept my way onto the set. Screw her! I rush toward her, balling my fist as I go. Before Maggie can blink, I pull back and drill her right in her nose with a crunch and splatter of blood. She sags back into Hudson. Pain explodes in my knuckles, and I realize I've never hit someone like that in my life. I shake out my hand, cussing and jumping around. Hudson holds tight to her but busts up laughing. About that time, I remember something important that hasn't been addressed.

"What did you give my mom?"

Maggie doesn't answer because she's still struggling to stand. That must have been a good hit. I move around her and open the door to her SUV. Mom's chest is rising and falling, but she's still asleep.

"Mom!" I shout into the vehicle. She doesn't budge so I turn to Maggie. "Tell me what you gave her!" I scream.

"She was already drunk. I didn't do that. With me she just smoked some good weed, had a snack and fell asleep. She's fine. She talks too much, but she's fine."

Although I'm pissed I relax a little because that's what Mom looks like when she's passed out from drinking or drugs. It's nothing new. I just want to make sure I don't need to take her to the ER.

Mike pulls his phone from his pocket and dials the police department. "Yeah, this is Mike Wade from Security Six. I've got Maggie Whitman in my custody. I need you to send a squad car to pick her up. I'll notify Agent Tandy of the FBI, so you can expect him to be in touch." He says a few more things before he hangs up the phone and glances at me. "I'm moving your mom to my truck. We can get her checked out at the hospital or take her home. Your call." I can tell he's still pissed at me, but I'm pissed at him, too, so I don't care.

"Home. I'm sure she's fine."

He stalks off to take care of her, and I move over to Simone. "I'm sorry about all this. I'm obviously not going to be able to finish the signing. I'll call you later."

I hug her, and she holds on tight and says in my ear, "Go easy on him. He was terrified. Love you, girly. Call me soon, okay?"

I nod.

The police show up, get our statements and haul Maggie away. Eventually the crowd moves back inside and we load up in the truck where my mom is still passed out. I'm sure she was already drunk we she smoked pot, and if that's the case she won't be awake for a while.

We stop by my Mom's house to tuck her into bed, where she wakes up briefly, mumbles in coherently and then proceeds goes right back to sleep. After that we head back to Security Six headquarters. Hudson leaves without going into the building. Mike takes me inside and pulls out his first aid kit. Then, without a word, scowl still on his face, he lifts me to the counter and begins to doctor my wounds. When he's done, he still hasn't said a word. He helps me down off the counter, turns and walks away from me. When I finally catch up to him, after taking my time, I hear him saying to Albert, "Yeah, she's okay. Agent Tandy knows about Cadieux and has already got someone on the way to his house. It doesn't surprise me that he's obsessed. Shit, I've been obsessed with her for half my life, too, but I'd never kidnap her. Sounds like he planned on her living out a porn career in his basement. The guy is a freak and he's got a fuck-ton of money, so I'm keeping her under lock and key until he's in FBI custody. Yeah. We'll be at my place. Call if you hear anything. I need to feed her and get her to bed early. It's been a long fucking day."

I walk back out to the main room in the warehouse to wait for him. I'm still pissed and not ready to discuss what an asshole I think he's being.

14

Mike

It doesn't take a genius to realize Summer's pissed off. Yelling at her probably wasn't the smartest thing to do in the middle of that mess and all those people, but there was no way I could tamp down the anger and fear that I felt when I realized what happened. I was only gone to the bathroom for a few minutes. It's a good thing Hudson was paying attention—not that I doubted him—or she might be gone with crazy Maggie.

We ride quietly to my place, and when we arrive, she continues the silent treatment. I need to end the standoff so I can hold her and reassure myself that she's okay. My gut is still churning with residual worry and even with anger, because I can't seem to control all the variables in this situation.

Now that we know who this guy is, I'm even more nervous. He's a big-time Hollywood director, and I can guarantee he owns a lot of property outside of the United States, which would make finding her difficult if he gets a hold of her. Why he used Wallace and Maggie, I have no idea, other than they were both connected to Summer in Shadow Key.

Once inside my house, she pushes inside the bathroom and closes the door behind her. I need to find a way to fix this, but I need to calm down first. Scooter trots out of one of the bedrooms, so I take him out back to use the bathroom. When I return to the kitchen, I spy a bottle of bourbon I bought at the beginning of my vacation next to the row of shot glasses. I flip one over, pour the amber liquid in the glass and pour it down my throat. Then I repeat the process once more, close the cabinet door and go wait outside the bathroom, impatient to talk to Summer. Scooter follows me and sits at my feet, facing the door waiting for Summer to greet him.

It feels like forever, but is probably only another five minutes, before she opens the door and jerks back, startled to find me there.

"We need to talk."

She tries to push past me and I grab her. Her eyes flare and then quickly narrow. "I don't feel like talking."

"That's not an option. I left you to stew all the way home. Now it's time to talk."

"Fine." She shakes free of my grip, pushes past me and stomps into the kitchen. "Then let's talk about what kind of asshole you are for yelling at me in front of a crowd in the middle of a crisis." Scooter, who followed her in from the hall, whines at her feet. She glances down and her expression softens. "Hey, Scooter, I missed you," she croons as she scratches behind his ears and down his back for a minute before standing and facing off with me again.

"I was wrong for doing that and I'm sorry. But I need you to look at this from my point of view. My only priority in life right now is to keep you safe. I gave you instructions that would ensure your safety long enough for me to take a piss and you ignored them. What was I supposed to do? Skip out after you and break into song when I realized you were still in the parking lot?"

"They had my mom!" she shouts.

I throw my hands up, exasperated. "Your no-good, piece-of-shit mom who has never had your back?"

"She's still my mom. She's all I've got." The last sentence is like a slap in the face, and I jerk back at her words. She takes a deep breath and her eyes widen, probably understanding what she's said. Scooter must understand that this is getting worse because he trots back to the bedroom leaving us to our argument.

"Are you kidding me? You've been part of our family since you showed up in a dirty blue sundress with crooked ponytails and bare feet. Are you saying we aren't there for you?" My fury peaks and boils over.

"That's not what I said. You know what I mean."

I shake my head and fight the urge to lose my shit. "No, I don't. Your mom hasn't thought of what's best for you one day in your life. You ate most meals with us, you went on vacation with us, you stayed at our house most nights. Unless you and Valerie got in a stupid tiff, you were with us. Now you're saying *she* is all you have?" I've closed in on her and she's craned her neck all the way back, studying me with wide eyes. It's possible I've finally gotten through, but now I'm so pissed I can't stand here and talk about it. I turn to storm out of the room and she grabs my arm and tugs.

"Wait! Wait! I'm sorry. Don't walk out, please. You don't get it and I don't expect you to since you grew up in such a great family. But I can't let something happen to her."

I twist back to glance at her and see that her eyes are filled with tears. Kryptonite. Her tears are my weakness and have been for years. Something her mom, along with that piece-of-shit sperm donor she calls a father, caused often.

I don't want to scare her, even as mad as I am, so I force my shoulders to relax. Then I continue to stare down at her, afraid that if I open my mouth something I'll regret will spill out. My fists stay clenched, though, because I'm still so angry.

Summer places both hands on my cheeks and stares at me as the tears leak down her face.

"Please don't be mad at me. Gladys will always be my mom, and I may not like her much, but I do love her. If I didn't, I wouldn't be the woman you think I am. Cut me some slack. I've never had to deal with this kind of thing before. I'm doing the best I can."

The pull to her is so strong, the need to comfort and protect her is even stronger, while the need to sink into her perfect, sweet little body is suddenly overwhelming. I need the physical reassurance that she's okay. I want to be close to her, as close as I can get and I need those things right now.

My head lowers and my mouth crashes into hers while I reach down to grip her thighs and lift her to sit on my kitchen table. I break the kiss, pull my shirt over my head and move just as quickly to get hers off. After that, it's a frenzy of lips, teeth, tongues, skin and hands, neither of us stopping until I'm buried deep and pumping away at her hot, sweet pussy. Although I feel like I can't get deep enough, the force of my thrusts moves the table across the room until it bangs into the wall. I'm leaning over her, braced on the table as she nips at my neck and chest with her teeth. The heels of her feet dig into my back. I increase the pace, and the smacking of our flesh mingled with her building moans is so damn hot.

The scent of our sex has taken over the room, sending my testosterone into overdrive. There is something about her that turns me into a caveman—taking away my ability to go slow and sweet. She shouts my name and arches her back, kneading her own tits. Her pussy clenches tight around me and she comes with my name on her lips, forcing me to explode inside her. My muscles relax instantly and I rest against her, both of us trying to catch our breath.

Once we settle a little and without breaking contact, I lift her up and carry her to my bathroom, stepping into the shower with her. She clings to me like I'm her lifeline, and in my heart, I know this is how it's supposed to be. Me loving her, me caring for her, and me protecting her at all costs. As I set her down under the spray, her eyes blink open, focusing on me.

Needing to make it right, I say, "I'm sorry I yelled at you and embarrassed you. But I'm not sorry for loving you enough to be angry about the whole situation." I smooth her hair down and ask, "Was I too rough just now? The sex, I mean."

"No, I like the sex however you give it, but yelling at me in front of everyone hurt my heart. I've had enough of that in my life; I don't want it from you."

I lean down and kiss her softly. "I'm sorry. You're right. I'll do my best to be more careful with your feelings."

We take our time washing and touching each other, me avoiding her scrapes, until the water runs cold.

As we're drying off, Summer turns toward the mirror to look at her backside. "I always thought you were a butt guy. I don't have one. I've got big boobs but no butt. Do I need to get implants or something? I don't want you leaving me one day for some woman with a famous round butt whom you're running security for."

What the heck is she talking about? I lean over and playfully bite her butt cheek. "Nope, it's the perfect size for biting." Then I move in close behind her, reaching around to palm her heavy breasts.

"These make up for any missing flesh on your ass. Been jerking off to the thought of these for years. I don't want or need anyone but you and what you come equipped with." I drop my hands from her breasts and watch as they bounce a little before I smack her ass playfully. "Come on, let's get you a shirt, some Neosporin for your scrapes and an ice pack for your knuckles. I'm ready to eat. Tomorrow morning, we'll get up and go by your house to get you some clothes."

LATER THAT EVENING, we lie on the couch and watch *The Goonies*—a movie we've always loved. Just after Andy accidentally kisses Mikey in the movie, my cell phone rings.

"Why do you have that old-school ringtone? It's so annoying," Summer complains. I roll my eyes at her and answer the phone.

"Hey, Roman," I say, noting the name on the screen.

"Hey, Mike. Sorry to bug you, but I wanted to give you an update. Jean-Christophe has disappeared. He was last seen at the Orlando airport but not since then. His car hasn't run through any tolls, it doesn't have LoJack and his phone's off. None of his known friends have seen him, so we're flying blind here. Make sure your security is tight until he resurfaces. Hudson is coming to sit outside your house in a nondescript black four-door sedan with dark windows. It's got a Florida tag. Keep your cell on you. If he sees anything, he'll call you."

"Thanks, Roman."

"No problem. Now I need to get some sleep. Call Albert or Amelia if you need anything; they're on call."

Roman disconnects and I realize that Summer's watching me carefully, trying to decipher if the news is good or bad.

I explain to her what was said, and she lays her head back down on my chest without a word.

"Look at me."

She lifts her eyes to mine, but says nothing.

"Everything is going to be okay. Tomorrow we're going to work out a plan to lure him in and nab his ass. I'm ready to move on with our lives together without fear running the show."

"I need to call Phil Harmon tomorrow. I have no idea what the studio will do since Maggie and the executive producer are in jail."

"Okay, let's finish our movie, then we'll go to bed and work it all out tomorrow."

———

THE NEXT MORNING I'm cooking eggs and bacon when Summer drifts out of my room. Her hair is a sexy mess and my T-shirt is so big it has slid over, exposing a shoulder as it tries to fall off her body.

"Morning, beautiful," I say, smiling at her. I'll never tire of the sight of her.

"Morning," she mumbles and rubs her eyes, moving in close to me.

"You hungry?"

"Nah, I need coffee first. I'm so tired. I couldn't sleep last night."

"Why not?" I ask. I fell right to sleep, but I don't often have problems sleeping.

"I was trying to think of a way to finish this off. I don't want to hide. I don't want to run, and I don't want to put my life on hold anymore. It's bad enough that my career didn't start until my 40s, but to have to pause it now too? No way. I'm ready to be done with this. Can't we dangle me like a carrot? Give me a tracking device, pepper spray, or a stun gun and put me under surveillance. I could even call him and set up a time to meet. I don't care how, but let's get this over with."

I set the spatula down on the counter and turn to fully face her. "There's no way in hell I'm dangling you in front of a crazy man. Any number of things could go wrong and I won't risk your safety like that. You're finally mine, and there's no way I'm letting you go."

She places her cool palms on my face and rubs her thumbs along the morning stubble on my jaw as she stares at me like she's contemplating something.

"Mike, I've waited my whole life to mean something to someone. To have a real connection, real love. I wouldn't risk anything about that if I thought there was a better way. You work for an elite protection agency with access to all the bells and whistles. If anyone can keep me safe, you and the rest of Six Security can. They've done everything possible up to now. Let's sit down with them today if they're available and see what they say. If we end this, we can get on with our lives . . . together."

Clenching my teeth, I consider what she's said. I know she's right, but it's taken me so long to get her that I don't want to risk it. I also know that anything can go wrong in even the best-planned operation. If something happens to her . . . I'll never be able to live with myself.

She's going to fight me on this and I don't want to argue this morning, so I push it off on my team. There's no way they're going to allow it. "Fine. We can talk to the team and see what they say, but I think they'll side with me on this."

"If they do then I'll accept that, but let's at least try. I want this to be over." She looks so desperate, and I can tell this is wearing on her more than she's letting show. I lean in, placing a quick but gentle kiss on her lips, and finish making breakfast.

―

MIDMORNING we arrive at Six Security headquarters to find Albert, Amelia, Roman, Randy and Hudson waiting for us. Everyone is in the conference room ready for a meeting. Roman, Amelia and Albert have laptop computers open in front of them, while Hudson has a yellow lined pad of paper and a pen. Randy has nothing but his coffee in front of him as he sits back with his legs stretched out, crossed at the ankles. This is as relaxed as he gets.

Summer's hand is in mine as we enter the room, and she

removes it to give a small wave. I pull out her chair for her and take a seat next to her, across the table from Albert and Amelia.

"Morning," Summer says, and the sound of her sweet voice makes me smile. I know I look like a swooning schmuck when she's near, but I can't seem to help it. When I focus again, Albert is studying me with an intensity that I'm not used to having aimed at me.

Before I get a chance to say anything, Summer speaks up. "Mike's not okay with this idea but agreed to let me run it past you. I want to be the bait that draws Jean-Christophe out. I feel like you guys could put a tracker on me in case something goes wrong and he snatches me. You could also give me pepper spray or something. I want this to be over, and I feel like we're at his mercy just sitting here waiting on him to make his move. My life is on hold indefinitely until he comes after me again. Everywhere I go, I'm on high alert. I can't sleep because I feel like a sitting duck. I need this to end one way or the other, and the easiest way to do that is to put me out there in the open where he can get to me. If we do it on our terms, you'll be guaranteed to have my back. If we wait for him to make his move, it could be when we're least prepared."

Everyone sits quietly, letting what she's said sink in. Amelia and Albert exchange a look that I can't decipher. To make sure they know my position, I reiterate my thoughts. "I don't like it. I think if we're patient, he'll come for her and we can handle it then."

Surprising everyone in the room, Hudson speaks up. "You aren't thinking clearly either. A man in love doesn't think with a tactical mind."

"I have more to lose than anyone here; I think I'm pretty clear on that."

Hudson, who is usually quiet speaks up. "Don't get defensive. We were taught to remove emotion from the situation, and you're the only one at the table who is understandably unable to do that. Summer's right. If we position her out front and center, but have everything in place—including a backup plan—then we control the situation instead of him controlling it. We already know he won't kill her. He wants her too bad for that."

"Don't be a dick. We both know there are worse things for women than death and this guy is capable of them, I think." It's easy for Hudson to be gung ho because the thought of another man touching Summer and forcing himself on her doesn't make him physically sick.

"Use your brain. If you think about it logically, you'll know this is the safest way to handle this situation. We get Summer set up for tracking, we arm her with something small but effective, and we call in the whole staff for this operation. Then we find somewhere for her to go out alone in public that has a minimum of exits so we can cover them. I can guarantee this guy will make a move. My gut says he's close by. We know he's totally lost it and is not thinking logically. If he sent Wallace and Maggie after her, who are as competent as Laurel and Hardy, then *he's* not thinking clearly. He's only thinking about grabbing Summer and going. We know his plane is in Orlando. We can also post someone on that. I've got a friend at the airport who can help us. I'm telling you, this is the best bet to end it. If she's willing, then we need to jump on this," says Hudson.

There is a long pause as everyone waits for Albert to chime in. He drums his fingers on the conference table as he contemplates this. Finally, he clears his throat. "I agree."

That is not what I expect him to say so I glare at him. "What if this were Amelia's life on the line?" I growl at him.

"She'd be able to take care of herself, but we aren't talking about Amelia. We're talking about Summer and she wants to do this. I imagine she'll follow our instructions to a T, and we'll arm her the best we can."

We all sit in another tense, uncomfortable silence until Randy finally says, "I get where you're coming from, Wade, but I also understand what Summer's saying. I had a similar situation with Ariel. Trust us to do our jobs, man."

Anger builds, pushing down on my chest, locking my muscles and clouding my thought process. I know I'm going to blow up and either become physically destructive or verbally assault my entire team. I'll regret that later, so I stand and leave the room. I respect everyone in there and I don't want to be an asshole, but I can feel it coming on like a freight train. Summer calls to me as I storm from the room.

A cadence of footsteps follows me from the conference room across the building, but I don't stop until I'm outside. I knew it wasn't Summer following me just by the heaviness of the steps, but I'm a little surprised when I turn to find Amelia coming through the door.

"Amelia—" I start, ready to ask for a few minutes to cool off.

She holds up a hand to stop me. "Let me say one thing before I leave you alone. As a woman, I understand the vulnerabilities you're talking about. As someone in love, I understand your need to protect. As your friend, I understand your fear, but you've got to trust us. We'd never do anything to harm anyone, especially a woman you love, and we have a team that's capable of handling an op like this. I agree with Summer. It's better to do this on our terms if she's willing to put herself out there. We could get it over with tomorrow if we do it right, assuming Cadiuex is as close and unhinged as we think he is. I agree with Hudson and think that he's just waiting for the perfect moment to grab her. Let's provide it and the means to end it."

My shoulders remain tense, but my anger is in check as I do my best to explain. "I know you're right, but I've waited almost my whole life to have Summer, and I don't want to give her up, especially in some horrific way." The things I've seen over the years flicker quickly through my mind like an awful horror movie.

"You won't. Trust us. Believe in your team." She pats my back before saying, "I'll leave you time to think," and walks back inside, her long brown ponytail swishing behind her.

15

Summer

I know Mike's mad and I understand why, but I'm suffocating in this situation. I need the freedom to live my life and I can't as long as this madman is stalking me. I find it hard to believe that a big-time French director has to resort to stalking to get a woman. There are thousands of beautiful younger women who would jump at the chance to do his movie. I could even refer about 20 to him in the next 10 minutes. I don't get why he's all over me. Hell, no one even knew my name until last year and for Hollywood standards, at 43 years old, I'm ancient. I just happen to fit a certain niche for now. In a year, this could all be different, and I could be back to waitressing. But I want to live this dream come true for as long as the industry will allow it. While this freak show is on the loose, I can't do anything and it pisses me off.

Amelia comes back inside and says, "I did my best. Now we wait. Summer, you can use the computer in my office if you'd like."

"I think I'll just wait here. He'll come back soon."

"Albert," Amelia says, turning to him, "why don't we work on a plan in case Mike caves on this. We need to look at a couple of possible locations." He nods and leads Amelia from the room with a hand at her hip. I sigh, a little jealous of how easy their affection is. Hudson and Randy follow, leaving me alone in the conference room. I pull up my social media accounts on my phone and scroll trying to keep my mind off of all of this until the door finally opens a half hour later and my big sexy protector comes through, his expression still dark like a rain cloud.

I stand up and face him, keeping a close eye on his expression. When the tightness around his eyes and mouth relaxes at my touch, I breathe a sigh of relief.

"Don't be mad at me," I whisper.

"I'm not mad at you. I'm scared and I'm not the kind of man who's okay with being afraid. Do you understand that I'm in love with you? And that my highest priority in life is making sure you're safe?"

Using my pointer finger, I trace his eyebrows, the slight slope of his nose and down across his lips. "Yes, I get it. I also understand that I'm in love with you, too, and I don't want to live under lock and key with you. I want everyone to know that you're my man. Your family, my crazy mother, our friends, our colleagues, the tabloids. Everyone. I don't want to hide inside anymore. Please do this so we can have this new life together without the threat looming in the background. I want to lie next to you at the beach and stare at that bronze six-pack blatantly instead of sneakily, now that I can. I want to fly out and see Val together and go as your girlfriend, not only as her best friend. We can end this. I trust your team to do this right."

He exhales and I can tell he's frustrated. I'm surprised when he says, "I know you're right, but this is hard for me. It goes against everything I believe. My job is to protect and keep people—especially those I love—from harm. I'll go along with this, but you're going to follow our guidelines. No going out on your own with this. I'm already freaked out about the whole thing as it is."

"I promise to do exactly as instructed. No more getting a note and going to save my mom. Please go into Albert's office and plan whatever it is that will help us end this."

———

WHILE THEY'RE PLANNING, I'm in Amelia's office back on social media and checking my email. When they still aren't done a couple hours later, I pull up solitaire on the computer and lose myself in the game. I should be afraid, considering this guy, Jean-Christophe, has proven to be totally crazy and creepy, but the safety I feel with Mike and the Security Six team is beyond compare. I need to trust their plan and not falter if Jean-Christophe pulls something unexpected. The guy is obviously capable of anything. I'm more freaked out than I'm letting on in front of Mike because I really believe this is the best way to end this quickly.

A couple of hours later, Mike comes back to find me. "Okay, you ready? The team should be here in a few minutes to discuss our plan of action and your role in it. We made it as simple as possible as far as you're concerned."

After a few minutes, everyone arrives and gets seated around the conference table again and Mike explains, "Amelia is taking you to dinner at the Parmesan Palace. That way it will look like a ladies' night out. I don't think he's dumb enough to believe I'd let you go out alone after all that has happened. We'll have someone on the front door, at each of the emergency exits, and the entrance to the kitchen. We're expecting Jean-Christophe to make a move when Amelia uses the bathroom near the end of dinner. If he doesn't take the bait, then we move the whole operation to your house and Amelia will leave after half an hour to give the appearance that you're alone. We've spoken to the manager so he knows we'll be running security covertly at the restaurant. He doesn't know the whole of what we plan to do, only that you'll be having dinner there and the team wants to blend in."

"That seems pretty elementary," I say. You don't think Jean-Christophe will see straight through that plan? After having you practically tied to me for the last week, I think he'll find it suspicious that you aren't with me. Hell, anyone who watches the old episodes of *21 Jump Street* would probably figure this whole thing out."

"The man is unhinged. He's not analyzing anything at this point. He's looking for an opportunity. I spoke to Jean-Christophe's assistant who told me that the last time she saw him, her boss hadn't showered in days and was muttering things to himself.

"What if that's an act?" I gnaw on my fingernail and fidget a little.

This time Albert chimes in. "If it is, we still have you under protection. We can go back to the drawing board tomorrow if he doesn't make a move today. We all feel like he's lingering, waiting for you to be alone for a few minutes."

"Okay, I'll do my part." I'm nervous but ready for this to be done. I'm also skeptical that it will be this easy. Nothing in my life has ever been easy.

At dinner time, I'm in the car with Amelia on my way to what I keep telling myself is a lovely Italian dinner with a friend. Twisting the feminine silver watch equipped with a tracking device on my wrist that Amelia gave me to wear makes me feel a little better. I do my best to push the nasty part of the whole thing out of my mind so I don't appear nervous. We're about to find out what kind of actress I really am.

Amelia pulls around the Parmesan Palace parking lot, circling the building twice slowly to make it look like she's searching for a spot up close, but part of the plan is to give

Jean-Christophe enough time to follow without issue. When we finally park four rows deep on the side of the restaurant, I do my best to ignore the chills dancing down my spine. They're probably imagined. We don't even know if Jean-Christophe followed us. I swallow down my fear, square my shoulders and exit the vehicle with Amelia following behind me to the restaurant.

The small talk we started while driving halts abruptly when Amelia makes a strange noise about 15 feet away from the car, and I turn to find her on the ground. The gash on her forehead makes me think she was hit with the shaky revolver that Jean-Christophe is now aiming at her unconscious body. Terror engulfs me when I realize he'll probably pull the trigger. The man has clearly lost it. I understand what his assistant was talking about it. Jean-Christophe's eyes are wild and flashing nervously from left to right. His hair is wild like some mad scientist in an old movie.

"I knew it wouldn't take long to get you once that asshole was gone. Let's go!" he barks in heavily accented English and gestures for me to turn in the other direction. With a quick glance down at Amelia again, I take in her closed eyes and limp form but relax slightly when I realize her chest is moving. At least I know she's alive. I go where he points, my stomach knotting tighter with each step. I slip my hand in my pocket and grip the pepper spray Mike gave me earlier. I might be able to use it if I can hold it right. I could run but that would leave Amelia vulnerable. I need to draw him away from her before I try to use the spray or escape. The guys were expecting this to happen in the Parmesan Palace, not in the parking lot right away. Will anyone realize how quickly things have changed?

There should be two people stationed inside the restaurant and two people arriving within five minutes after me and Amelia, but there's no one out here now. Jean-Christophe and I will be gone by the time anyone figures out what happened, and worse, I couldn't tell if Amelia was dying or just knocked out. She was lying motionless between two cars, and I can't help but worry.

With the gun at the small of my back, Jean-Christophe guides me over several rows to a black sports car with dark-tinted windows. He yanks the door open, urging me inside, and the panic rising inside forces my fight or flight instinct to kick in. There's no freaking way I'm getting in that car. I turn as quick as I can and throw a wild punch, missing his jaw but stunning him enough that he doesn't move out of the way completely, and I nail him in the throat. Gasping and choking, he drops the gun and stumbles back a little bumping into the car behind him. "Bitch," he wheezes.

I point the pepper spray his way and push the button. He screams and flails more so I drop the spray and scramble away, bending low and running as fast as I can through the parked cars, not caring where I'm going, only that I get away. I need to get to the restaurant, to people who can help me. He must have recovered quickly because I can hear his feet pounding the pavement behind me.

"You stupid bitch!" he screams as he chases me. I turn left and cut through the next row of cars. I rise a little and glance back to figure out where he is, and the window next to my head shatters as a bullet whizzes past. So much for thinking he won't kill me.

I scream and drop low, crawling along the ground in my attempt to get away from the car he just shot. Jean-Christophe knows I'm over here, but I have no idea where he is. I climb to my feet but stay crouched down and do my best to listen for his footsteps. My blood is roaring through my system at full force, and it sounds like a raging river in my ears as the adrenaline continues to pour through my body. Anger seems to push up from my toes building as it rises, slowly pushing aside the fear. There's no way I'm allowing him to take my happiness or life when I'm finally where I want to be. I haven't made him any promises so he has no right to me. His feet appear under the rear bumper of the car I'm behind, and I've had just long enough to go from running in fear to full fighting mode. He has no idea what's coming.

I spring to my feet and run toward Jean-Christophe screaming like a banshee—all the fear, frustration and anger comes out in that sound. I'm using everything I have pent up inside me to go berserk on him. The impact of my body connecting with his forces him to drop the gun. It bounces once and slides under the car I pin him to. I'm kicking, punching and clawing at him, trapping him in place. All he can do is cover his face and try to avoid my flailing limbs. Jean-Christophe clearly never expected me to be a fighter. I must get one good knee-shot to the groin because I feel the scab on my knee peel, and he doubles over while I pause to catch my breath, taking a few steps back to retreat. He stands back up and smirks at me, his eyes red and watery from the pepper spray and I realize I didn't get him in the balls. It was a trick to get me to stop attacking him.

The anger in my body explodes again at his arrogance. Another war cry comes from deep within and I charge him, tucking my shoulder into his gut like a linebacker, shoving him all the way back and smacking him into the car in the next row. His elbow comes down hard on my back and I stumble backward, breathless. Damn that hurt.

"You're mine! Quit fighting me!" Jean-Christophe screams, his French accent thick as he grabs my hair and forces my face upward to look into his crazed eyes.

As I'm assessing the situation for my next move, Mike pops up from behind the car and slowly creeps toward my psychotic captor. Mike hasn't drawn his attention, so I do my best to focus on Jean-Christophe, feeling the spit droplets hit my face as he growls, "*Cela a pris trop de temps.*" *This has taken too long.*

In a move I don't anticipate, Jean-Christophe's mouth crashes to mine roughly and I attempt to recoil, but he holds me in place by the hair. Just as I'm biting down hard on his tongue, he drops away from me to the pavement. Because he's slow to release my hair, I'm tugged down with him, leaning over his knocked-out form. His fingers go limp and release me, and I scramble backward and stand up straight. When I see Mike's okay, I breathe a sigh of relief. He lifts his sneakered foot and rests it on Jean-Christophe's chest as he pulls me against him, kissing the top of my head without a word. Then he pushes me away. "Stand over there in case he wakes up."

Shakily, I do as I'm told. The adrenaline that helped me survive the last few minutes is subsiding, and the thought of sitting down in the middle of the lot to regroup is almost too much to ignore, but I fight to stay standing.

In less than a minute, the parking lot is swarming with police, restaurant customers, and people from nearby businesses. Mike shoves his 9mm into the back of his jeans and lifts his hands in the air as the police approach cautiously, guns aimed at us. I turn toward them fully reach out toward Mike and yell, "It's okay, this guy is okay." I then point down at Jean-Christophe. "The man on the ground is my stalker."

Mike and I spend a long time answering questions for the police and being looked at by the EMTs on the scene. When Jean-Christophe finally comes to, he's cuffed and sent to jail after a brief once-over by the paramedics. By the time we get back to Mike's house, I'm exhausted and sore in too many places to count. He lets Scooter out to go to the bathroom, and I change into one of his T-shirts.

When Scooter comes trotting back inside, I scoop him up and place him in my lap while I get comfortable on the couch. Mike drops down beside me and drapes an arm over my shoulder, and we sit like this for a long time, watching some old game show on TV. I don't think either of us are really paying attention to what's on, but it's nice to focus on absolutely nothing for a change.

———

THE NEXT MORNING, I wake up to find it's only me and Scooter in the house. A note on the counter next to a warm pot of coffee indicates that Mike had to run to the store and will be back soon. After I drink a cup, I take a quick shower and do some first aid on my reopened skinned knee. Then I sit on the back porch, relaxing and trying to come to terms with everything as Scooter sniffs what looks like the entire backyard.

"M!" Mike shouts as he slams the front door. I stand and lean my head inside.

"I'm out here with Scooter."

When he reaches me he kisses me long and hard. He's happy about something. "Looks like you already showered. I was hoping to join you," he tells me with a boyish grin.

"Too late," I tease and sit back in the rocking chair I was occupying before he came home.

"Have you called your director today?"

"I called before my shower. Filming is postponed for six weeks."

"Good, you can go with me to Colorado to surprise Thea for her birthday in three weeks."

I think about it for a second and realize I have no reason to say no. Although I'd love to see Mike's sister Valerie and his niece Thea I'm a little concerned about what Val say about my relationship with Mike. I hate hiding anything from her and would love to share with her, but what if she freaks out? That's not really her style, but I've also never had to tell her that I'm in love with her brother. It may make the dynamic between the three of us weird too. Considering my mom is such a screwup, their family is the only one I have. If this upsets her, I don't know what I'll do.

"Why are your eyebrows scrunched up?" Mike asks as he leans in and runs his thumbs over them, smoothing them down.

"What if Val gets upset?"

He stands up and crosses his arms over his chest. "Why would she?"

"I don't know, but we used to be . . . I don't know. A group? Now, we'd be a couple plus her. Won't that be weird?"

"You don't think she'll be happy for us?"

I shrug and look away, not wanting to contemplate Val's response. "I don't know after everything she's been through."

"Val loves you. She loves me and she's always wanted us to be happy, like we want her to be. It's going to be okay. I promise. Trust me, please." He pulls me out of my seat and wraps his arms around me. "Don't worry, things will only change for the better."

16

Mike

It's been five weeks since Summer and I became an item. As I suspected, Valerie was thrilled about our new status as a couple and since our visit to see her, Summer has relaxed even more into our relationship. I had a weeklong assignment out of state right after we returned from Colorado and just got back home last night. Every day Summer and I talked on the phone at whatever time I had available and she stayed with Scooter. Now we only have one week together before she has to return to Key West to shoot, and she's been quiet. I'm not ready for her to leave yet and I'm hoping that's her issue too. The one week apart was too much for me, but I didn't say anything because I know she's afraid that's what will end us.

"M, you about ready?" I ask, leaning in the doorway to the bathroom, anxious to leave for our visit with my grandparents. There's more to tonight, but she doesn't have a clue.

"Yes, let me put on my lips," she says, just like she always does before she puts her lipstick on.

Once she's done, I lead her out to the truck, opening the door and helping her inside. By the time we reach my grandparents' house, my palms are a little sweaty so I wipe them on my jeans.

"Why are you nervous?" she asks as I'm opening the door.

"What?" My mind is so muddled with what's about to happen that I don't know what to say.

"You're nervous. Your palms sweat when you're nervous. They always have, since we were kids. Remember the time you had to sing that solo in elementary school and when they passed you the mic, your hand was so sweaty the mic slid right through and bounced on the ground, causing that awful sound and making half the audience go deaf?"

"How the hell do you remember stuff like that?" I ask her.

"I pay attention, that's all. Besides, that was funny as hell." She giggles a little and I get out of the jeep, not wanting to explain what the issue is. When I come around to her side of the truck, she's already gotten out so I shut her door, but instead of taking her inside my grandparents' house, I lead her to the middle of the front yard and stop dead.

"What are you doing? Why are we standing in the grass? Your granny is waiting on us."

"No, she's not." I take both of Summer's hands in mine and hold them lightly, aware of my sweaty palms. When she looks up at me, her blue eyes watch me intently.

"I brought you here because I'm feeling really sentimental. This exact spot is where I was standing 35 and a half years ago when you came into the yard looking for new friends." Her eyebrows draw together like she's thinking about what I've said. "Your hair was in two uneven, fuzzy pigtails, you had on a blue sundress with one strap that kept falling off, and you had dirt on your hands and bare feet. I thought you looked like a dirty little angel. From that day forward, you've been part of my life. It didn't matter how far I went or how long I was gone. It didn't matter who I was dating or who you were dating. We kept our friendship alive, and it's the most precious thing in my life. Or at least I thought it was, until I kissed you that first time after our Colorado trip. There's not another woman on this earth that I want to spend the rest of my life with. I thought about waiting a little longer to ask, because this part of our relationship is new, but I don't need to. I knew I loved you long before our first kiss, so I refuse to waste any more time." I lower myself to one knee and pull the little blue velvet box from my pocket. As I pop it open, I watch the first tear slide down her face and my nerves kick up another notch. *Please don't say no,* I chant over and over in my head.

"Summer Jessica Arden, will you marry me?"

She's silent as the tears run down her face, and my stomach is clenched up tight. Is she about to break my heart?

She reaches out and places her hands on my jaw and runs her thumbs over my cheeks. "Yes," she says, her voice scratchy with emotion. I pull the marquise-cut diamond ring from the box and slip it on her ring finger. The tears continue down her face, and before I can stand, she says, "I have something to tell you." She swipes at her river of tears and ends up smearing them rather than wiping them away. After a big swallow, she says, "We're gonna have a baby."

I blink up at her. "What?"

"A baby. We're gonna have a baby."

I look down at her stomach and back to her face. She's smiling and sniffling.

"Really?" I ask, unable to believe this is happening.

"Yes, I found out while you were gone and I was afraid to tell you. I was worried you'd think I was trying to trap you."

"Trap me? I'm more likely to trap you than vice versa."

"Yes. We have some things to talk about. Big things, but yes. You're going to be a daddy."

I leap up from the ground and grab her around the waist, spinning her as we go. She squeals with delight and smacks me on the shoulder. "I'm gonna puke. Cut it out!"

I set her down gently and kiss her with everything I have until a loud whistle cuts through the fog of happiness.

"Boy, get a room. My front yard ain't the Holiday Inn," my granddad yells.

"She said yes," I yell back.

"Well, duh!" he yells back to me.

"And she's going to have my baby too!"

"Well, get her in here so we can feed her!" Granny hollers, and we both laugh.

Wrapping Summer in my arms, I kiss her hair, so thankful for this whole evening. In the middle of my bliss, an unwelcome thought occurs to me. "You have to go back to Key West and pick up a crazy schedule. I don't want you to give up your new career, but I'm going to worry."

"I already thought of that. I talked to my agent while you were gone and asked to add security detail to my expenses. An actress I worked with did that. Granted, she was a bigger name than I am, but with everything that happened, my agent didn't think I'd have a problem getting that negotiated in."

"You're going to have a bodyguard?"

"Yes, I thought that might make you feel better."

"Yeah, but no one is guarding this body but me."

"I already thought of that too. I contacted Amelia yesterday about contracting you through Security Six, at least until the baby is born."

"What did she say? She didn't mention anything to me when I talked to her earlier."

"I asked her to let me talk to you about it. She said they'd be willing to do it if it's what you want. I know you love your job, and if you want to keep doing it, I'll interview and hire someone else until I deliver. Then we can revisit everything. I don't want you to stop doing what you love to follow me around, but I didn't want to take the option from you either."

"So, you're asking me to be your bodyguard?"

"Well, yeah." Summer looks at the ground like she's afraid to see my face when I respond.

"You want me on location with you and tied to you that tight?"

"Of course. There's no one I want more, but if it's too mu—"

"That's not even a question, M. I love you. I've waited for this too many years to count. I'll follow you wherever you want to go."

She looks at me with tears in her eyes. "What if you get tired of me? My own mother can't even . . ."

"Don't take this the wrong way, but your mother is a selfish cow. She never loved you like you deserved to be loved, and now that I have a chance to show you how good it can be, I'll do it. Our baby won't experience a single second of what you felt growing up. There is nothing more important than you, this baby and our future together. I love you." Before she can respond, I kiss her softly, my lips lingering longer than normal, willing her to feel the truth behind my words.

My granddad, being the cantankerous old man he is, breaks the moment by yelling, "Boy! If you don't get that girl in here and feed her so she can grow my great grandbaby, I'm gonna take a switch to your butt." Summer and I both bust up laughing again because we were threatened as kids with the "switch" when we'd get too rowdy, but he never could do it.

"Okay, okay, Granddad, we're coming."

She slides her arm around my waist and my arm slips over her shoulder, holding her to me as we walk toward the front door. When we reach Granddad, he has a big smile. He lifts both hands, patting us each on a cheek. "Proud of you two. Glad you finally figured it out." We don't get the chance to respond because he turns on his heel and disappears into the house.

17

Mike

Albert and Amelia are sitting across from me in the conference room ready to discuss the changes in my life and possibly my career. I've spent the last two days since Summer said yes thinking about my future, and I'd like to make some adjustments now before the baby gets here.

"You two have been amazing. I can't get over how flexible and understanding you are with everything. I've been evaluating life and want to approach Summer about moving a little bit north. Raising our baby where life is a little slower feels like the right thing to do."

"Where are you thinking?" Amelia asks.

"Crystal River. It's only a little over an hour from the Tampa airport, so I can still get to jobs in a timely fashion if I need to leave town, but it's away from city life. I love Tampa, but I like the small town feel up there. Plus, we can be right on the water."

"Do you want to stay with Six Security, or are you planning on going out on your own?"

"I wouldn't do that to you guys. You've been supportive through everything."

They glance at each other, and Amelia nods at Albert before he looks back to me. "We've had an influx of applicants recently and have been considering taking on more employees. Although we'd love to keep you here with us, we've discussed it and are willing to release you from your contract if you'd like to go out on your own. Assuming you wouldn't bid against us for jobs, of course. At the time, when Amelia and I started discussing this, the only thing we knew was that Summer's contract was going to provide for a bodyguard and you could get a paycheck that way. However, with the new development of you moving out of the immediate area, it may be the right time to start your own business. Your whole life is changing so starting a new business may be too much of a risk, but we want you to know that we wouldn't hold any ill will if you chose this time to make your employment change. If we didn't have qualified applicants, this wouldn't be as easy to offer. As it is, if you decide to go out on your own, you'll be missed, but we understand the need for change and adjustment."

"Wow. This is not how I expected this conversation to go. Can you give me a little time to think about it? I need to talk to Summer, and see what she thinks. I'll get back to you. Thank you for giving me options." I stand and shake their hands and stride out of the room.

That's not at all how I expected that to go, but I can't say the possibility of going out on my own hasn't crossed my mind. After all Albert and Amelia have done for me, though, I didn't want to do anything that felt like a slap in the face to them. Since they are making the offer on their own, it would be stupid for me not to consider it.

⎯⎯

SCOOTER and I are in the kitchen, me drinking a bottle of water, contemplating what the best move for my family will be, while he sniffs every square inch of tile floor looking for a crumb of food he thinks might be there when Summer breezes into the house.

"We found it! Your mom and I found the perfect dress for the wedding. No big bows, no fluffy tulle . . . it's perfect! Exactly what I wanted!" she yells from the entryway.

I step out of the kitchen to greet her, and she drops her purse on the table moving toward me. "Well, where is it?" I ask, smiling at her as I pull her in close to me and link my fingers together at the small of her back.

"You can't see it until the day of the wedding! That's bad luck! Your mom has it in the perfect hiding spot."

I chuckle, loving the sound of happiness in her voice.

"Val called while I was finishing up at the dress shop. She's trying to get her schedule switched to be here for it. Maybe we should change the date so it's not so hard on her. I didn't even think about it being difficult for her to get off of work on short notice."

"Valerie will be here. If not, you and I can go back out to see her and Thea before our baby comes after you're finished shooting *Shadow Key*. Don't worry about it for now. Listen, we need to sit down and talk for a few minutes."

I release her and move over to the table to have a seat. She stands where I left her, twisting a lock of hair around her finger nervously.

"Hey, don't be nervous. It's just something we need to discuss. It's not bad."

With a little nod, she moves over to sit in the chair next to me adjusting it to face me. "What's up?"

"You know I met with Albert and Amelia today right?"

"Yeah," she answers cautiously.

"They offered to let me out of my contract so I could go out on my own."

"What? Why? That doesn't make sense. You're the best they have."

"Well, with the offer to be your bodyguard and our lives changing the way they are, they thought it might be a better situation for us. I mentioned to them that I'd like to move to the Crystal River area sometime soon. The idea of raising our baby here doesn't appeal to me. If we go up there, we could use the Suncoast Parkway to get to the Tampa airport in about an hour. Here, we're close enough to see our family often, but life is slower up there. Of course, if you don't want to do that, we don't have to. I just want you to consider it. If we're moving to Crystal River, it makes more sense for me to go out on my own. If we stay in Tampa, it's a crapshoot which is the better option."

"As long as I'm with you, I don't care where we live. I don't want to go far from your family, and it would help to be relatively close to an airport, but an hour is nothing. Other than those couple of things, I'm leaving it up to you."

"Making this decision with you is important. I don't want to decide the fate of our family alone."

"I already told you the three things that matter to me. Being with you, driving distance to your family and an airport. Other than those . . . I don't care what we do."

18

Mike

One month later . . .

Out by the lake on my grandparents property, at five minutes after six o'clock in the evening, a handful of guests are seated in white folding chairs we had delivered this morning for the occasion. My brother Thomas is on one side of me and the judge we found to perform the ceremony is on the other. As a surprise for Summer, I flew my sister Valerie, my niece Thea and Valerie's boyfriend Javier in for the wedding. They should have arrived about 15 minutes ago so I'm wondering if that's what's causing the delay.

Just as I'm about to abandon my spot in front of everyone to see what's taking so long, Javier strides out from the doors leading to where Summer has been getting ready. The grin on his face is huge. He comes right up to shake my hand and give me a half-hug.

"Good to see you, man. The girls will be out in a minute. Val couldn't wait, so they went straight to the dressing room. Congratulations!"

"Thanks, I was starting to get nervous that y'all weren't going to make it."

"My girls had to change into their dresses at the airport. Then it took us a few minutes to get a cab." Javier leans over and shakes hands with Thomas as I introduce them. Considering the small group we have gathered, I announce, "Hey, guys. This is Valerie's man, Javier. They're here. It should only be a minute or two longer." Javier shakes hands with everyone and then takes the seat next to Summer's friend Simone. A few minutes later Thea comes through the door in a pretty light-pink dress, followed by her mother, Valerie, who still looks teary-eyed and is smiling widely at me. They both rush to me, and I wrap an arm around each of them and kiss their foreheads.

"Thanks for coming," I choke out as I fight back the tears.

"We wouldn't miss it," Val says.

"No way! This is awesome," Thea chimes in happily.

Before I can say anything more, the door opens and Summer comes through on my Dad's arm. She's wearing sky-high heels and a short white beaded dress that skims her curves without clinging too tightly. White and red gerbera daisies make up her small bouquet, and I can't help but grin at her. When she gets to the edge of the concrete walk way, she stops and kicks off her shoes and continues through the sand barefoot to stand next to me.

My dad places her hand in mine, kisses her cheek and slides into the chair next to my mom in the front row with Scooter at their feet. I guide her to stand in front of me and say, "God, you're beautiful, M."

She flaps her hand in front of her face like she might cry again, so I squeeze her hand and turn to the judge. "We're ready."

He adjusts his glasses and reads the prepared script. I tip Summer's face up to look at mine, wanting to stare into her sapphire depths through this whole thing. I want to burn this moment so deep into my memory that it never goes away.

After we've been declared husband and wife and have spent the evening enjoying dinner with our family and friends, I finally excuse us from the group. I'm ready to go to the hotel room and show my gorgeous new wife just how happy she makes me.

THREE MONTHS LATER . . .

My phone rings as Summer and I sit in the waiting room of the ob-gyn office ready to do the ultrasound to find out the sex of the baby. I glance at the caller ID and see it's Hudson.

Summer places her hand on my arm. "Go out in the hall and take it. By the looks of this waiting room, it's going to be awhile before we get our turn. I'll come get you if they call for me."

I nod and answer it as I step outside.

"What's up, man?"

"Nothing, you busy?"

"I'm at the doctor waiting for Summer's ultrasound, but it's crazy in there. I think I have a few minutes. What's up?"

"You still planning to go out on your own?"

"Yeah. Why?"

"Want a partner? My contract's up with Security Six, and I've been staying up in Crystal River in a house on the north end of town. I have no intention of leaving here any time soon, and I have the cash to buy into the business. If you don't think that's what you want, it's okay, but I'd like you to consider it."

"What about the noncompete with Albert and Amelia?"

"Because it's you, they're willing to waive that as long as I stick to the "not bidding against them for jobs" stipulation. They were cool about it. Look, I just want you to think about it. If it's not what you want, we'll still be cool, but with you starting a new family, it might help to have a partner that can be flexible with his time. Like I said, just think about it. I'm going to let you go so you can get back to Summer."

"All right, man, let me think about it and talk to my wife. I'll get back to you soon. Take care."

"You too," Hudson says and then disconnects.

When I return to the waiting room, Summer is playing solitare on her phone. She glances up at me. "How you feeling?" I ask as I reach out to touch the small baby bump that she conceals well with a baggy shirt.

"Good, but I have to pee and I can't until this is over. I wish they would hurry up. What did Hudson want?"

"He wants to go into business with me. He's been staying in Crystal River. His contract ended with Security Six and now he's ready for something new."

"What did you say?" She angles her body to face me a little more and waits for my answer.

"I told him I would think about it and talk to you."

"It might be helpful to have a partner like him, and we both know he's good at his job. I think it's worth considering."

I sit back and contemplate the idea of taking Hudson on as a partner while we wait.

Twenty minutes later, the ultrasound tech opens the door and calls out, "Summer Wade." We stand and follow her into the doctor's office. The tech guides Summer up to the table and helps her to lie back. Then tells her, "Pull your shorts down very low on your hips and your shirt up." After Summer does as she's told, the tech tucks a paper covering around her shorts to keep the ultrasound jelly from getting all over Summer's clothes. The tech flips the monitor on, grabs the wand and starts spreading the goo around as she presses buttons on her keyboard. Finally, on the monitor, a round head shape comes into view, and right after the rest of the body seems to appear. Little ribs and spine, arms, legs, the whole thing. It's crazy that only a couple of short months ago all we could see was a beating heart.

Summer sniffles and I glance up at her. "What's wrong?"

"I'm sorry. I'm so hormonal, but I just never thought I'd get this—especially with you. That's our baby. I'm so happy."

I wipe a tear from her cheek and tell the truth. "Me too."

The tech takes the time to do all the measurements and tell us that everything looks good.

Do you want to know what it is?" she asks.

Summer glances at me and I nod. "Yes," we say in unison.

The tech moves the wand around until the only thing I can identify is an alien-looking head. "We are looking from the bottom up, that's why the head looks distorted." She circles a little area. "That right there, or more accurately, the lack of that shows me you are having a little girl."

Now it's my turn to tear up. "A girl? Are you sure?"

"Yes, Mr. Wade."

"Now I have two beautiful girls to love and protect, Lord help me." I say with a smile. I couldn't be happier.

A WEEK HAS PASSED since we had the ultrasound. We moved the last of our stuff into the rental house on Crystal River two days ago with the help of my dad, Hudson and my brother. Tonight, we're having Hudson over to discuss the details of the partnership. Summer ordered food from the Lobster Lounge and has gone to pick it up. Hudson arrived about 15 minutes ago, and after some small talk, we're getting down to the nitty gritty.

"Sunset Security?" Hudson asks.

"That's what I was thinking. Summer and I tried a hundred different options for clever names, but they all just seemed lame. Do you have anything else you think would work better?"

"Nah, Sunset Security is fine with me."

Now that we have the name out of the way, we spend the next hour discussing pertinent details and planning to meet with a lawyer to draw up the contract and fill out any necessary paperwork. Summer comes home with dinner, and we continue to discuss the birth of not only our little girl but also of Sunset Security.

I glance around the room at the various boxes we still haven't unpacked. Then over at Scooter who is planted by the sliding-glass door, looking out at the passing boats on the river. Next, over to Hudson who is grinning like a lunatic, and then down at my wife stretched out next to me with her head on my thigh, laughing uncontrollably at something Hudson said. Finally, I stop on her little round belly, barely out, poking against her spandex pants. All of these changes in my life are happening simultaneously. Never have I been so happy, nor has my future seemed so bright or exciting. I'm a lucky man.

THE END

To contact Tiffani Lynn, sign up for her newsletter or find more of her steamy reads visit Tiffanilynn.com

SAVING STACEY: Florida Veterans Two

On the run from her abusive ex, Stacey Allen spends her days refilling coffee and wiping down tables, instead of using her finance degree crunching numbers. A low profile life is the only way to survive as she struggles to divorce her cheating husband. Having nowhere else to turn when trouble tracks her down, she accepts help from a mysterious stranger.

Former Navy SEAL Hudson McCormick spends his days as co-owner of Sunset Security and his nights bailing his drug addict ex-wife out of bad situations, including one that leads him to a damsel-in-distress. He can't help but be drawn to a woman in need, even if he doesn't want to be.

The longer she stays hidden away in the sleepy vacation town from her childhood, the more she realizes how much she loves the simple life and the more her feelings for Hudson grow. Just when Stacey starts to feel safe, his past collides with hers, putting them both in danger. Hudson will do whatever it takes to save Stacey - even if it means risking his heart.

49716038R00083

Made in the USA
Columbia, SC
28 January 2019